Pucked in

the Head

Thin Ice #2

Charity Parkerson

COPYRIGHT

or encourage electronic piracy of copyrighted materials. Brief passages may be quoted for review purposes if credit is given to the copyright holder. Your support of the author's rights is appreciated. Any resemblances to person(s) living or dead, is completely coincidental. All items contained within this novel are products of the author's imagination.

—Warning: This book is intended for readers over the age of 18. Some of my books contain allusions to past abuse and trauma.

CONTENTS

Introduction

*CATO'S BROKEN HEART COST **him everything. Now he has a second chance at
the top. Too bad his stupid heart plans
to test him again.***

After years of playing professional hockey in California, Cato has been traded after a less than stellar year. In his defense,
Cato spent the season watching the man
he loves fall in love with his twin. Now
he's nearly two thousand miles from his
brother and new brother-in-law. He has

a chance with a new team to be the star player again. Unfortunately, there's this other guy. It's a shame Cato needs everyone to believe he's straight.

Brodie has spent his life surrounded by hockey players. As the equipment manager for the Chuckers, there are a few things he knows for sure. Hockey players are loud, rough, stinky, and straight... even if they aren't. Very few hockey players live their truth before retirement. He learned a long time ago to steer clear of them. Brodie won't live in the closet. Now there's this new player.

Pucked in the Head is the second book in Charity Parkerson's Thin Ice series. These books are steamy sports romances meant to heat up your day.

CHAPTER ONE

PEOPLE DIDN'T SEE THE player side of things when they were forced from one team to another. These guys had been Cato's opponents. Now they were his teammates. Cato would eventually play against his old teammates, who were now his opponents. It fucked with the head. At least Cato still had ice beneath his skates. His best years weren't behind him yet. He recognized this trade for the second chance it was. Cato wouldn't fuck it up.

With two months left until the season started, Cato had a ton of shit to do. Moving his entire life from California to New Orleans had been a huge pain in the ass. He had found a house. Movers had dumped everything inside. Each time Cato looked at all the packed boxes, he found something else to do. It just seemed like such a momentous task. In another bid at procrastination, Cato had an appointment with his new agent.

Cato blew out a whistle at the first sight of Kieran Steele's house. Just outside the French Quarter, the place was massive and private, kept secret by a hidden courtyard. The house was a stark reminder of who really made the big bucks in sports. Of course, Kieran was worth it. He managed the best.

When Cato rang the doorbell, he half expected a butler to answer. That was how fancy the place looked. Then a face Cato recognized opened the door. They didn't know each other, but Henley Steele had played for the Chuckers too before his retirement. Everyone knew him.

"Hey. You must be Cato."

Cato smiled. "That's me."

Henley motioned with his head for Cato to come inside. "Kieran is waiting."

Cato stepped through the door. "You're Henley, right?"

Henley flashed him a smile. "Yep, that's me. I'm Kieran's husband."

The fact that Henley introduced himself as Kieran's husband and nothing more said a lot about their love. Henley didn't care to be recognized as anything more than Kieran's spouse. Cato would never find that.

"I hear you're the next biggest thing for the Chuckers."

God, he hoped that was true. Cato didn't want to go out being mediocre. "That used to be your title, if I recall."

Henley snorted. "I had my day. Now I have a shoulder that doesn't work right and never stops hurting. A knee replacement and less than half my real teeth."

"You still wouldn't trade it for the world."

Henley looked his way as he led Cato through the house. A bright smile stretched his lips. "I still wouldn't trade it for the world."

They shared a moment that only people with big dreams understood. After a second, he opened a door. Kieran sat behind a desk, staring at a computer screen. He looked up as Cato stepped inside the room. His gaze immediately shifted to his husband, as if it was out of his control. A wicked smile touched Kieran's lips. Cato experienced a moment of jealousy. He would bet everything he owned the pair had a scorching sex life.

Kieran finally focused on him. "Thank you for being on time."

"I'm eager to get started. I'd hate to get rusty during the off season."

Kieran nodded. "That's why I've called in a favor. The Chuckers' equipment manager, Brodie West, is one of the few people with full-time access to the arena. He's agreed to allow you to join him during working hours, as long as there are no other events being held. I'm expecting him any minute. You can go with him and get started today. Two major brands have already made offers to pay you a ridiculous amount to wear their gear on the ice. Both deals are equally attractive. Choose one and get your practice in."

"Thanks for that. I'm not used to going this long off the ice, but the move has been hectic."

"Just protecting my investment."

The door opened again.

Cato turned. He didn't know what he had been expecting. Maybe the same middle-aged ex hockey player that had been in charge of the Ice Rockets' equipment. Instead, Brodie turned out to be a guy likely in his mid-twenties. His dark hair looked soft and wild. Fuck. His face was perfect hard lines. His eyes were an odd shade of hazel Cato had never seen before. They were twice as beautiful, lined in dark eyeliner. His full lips had a light color smeared on them, highlighting them. A tattoo covered his neck, making Cato long to see how far down his body it went. His ripped black jeans and t-shirt made him look like he should be on the cover of some metal band's album. He was also all smiles.

Brodie held his hand out for Cato to shake. "Cato Janssen. I've followed your career."

Cato accepted the half hand clasp handshake thing friends did. It caught him off guard, but equipment manager was an important member of the team. It was best they formed a bond now. "I'm looking forward to working with you. Kieran was just telling me about you agreeing to help me out. I can't tell you how much I appreciate it."

Brodie winked and smiled. He had gorgeous teeth. It was such an odd thought, but damn. The guy was hot. "It benefits everyone, for you to be ready for the season. Are you ready to head out?"

Cato tossed a look Kieran's way. He had already gone back to staring at his computer screen like they were forgotten. Cato hadn't planned to get on the ice today, only check out the facility, but he was game. He met Brodie's stare again. "Sure."

Brodie nodded. "I'll drive. Kier and Hen don't care if your car stays here."

Kier and Hen? That sounded like friends.

"Cool. Lead the way."

Brodie turned away and Cato forgot to say his goodbyes. His gaze landed on the most perfect ass Cato had ever seen. He nearly whimpered. Cato had to behave.

Brodie led him outside to a waiting Jeep. The top and doors were missing. Cato climbed into the passenger seat. He tried to find something to talk about. "How long have you been with the team?"

Brodie popped on some sunglasses and looked Cato's way. It didn't make sense, but he got hotter by the second. "All my life." He circled the driveway and headed out the gate. Brodie explained as he drove. "My dad is Will West."

Cato nearly gasped. Everyone who had ever heard of hockey knew Will's name. He was the single greatest all-time player, and he had played for the Chuckers.

"Holy shit. Your dad is amazing. I've studied all his moves, trying to learn all his tricks."

Brodie nodded, but kept his gaze locked on the road. "That's what everyone tells me. My whole life, he's just been Dad. Everything in my life that involved hockey was just me hanging out with Dad while he trained. He showed me how to take care of all the equipment, but he never wanted me to play. Dad said he had already made the money, so I wouldn't have to. He had ruined his body, so I wouldn't have to. That was the one rule he was adamant I followed. But I still fell in love with the game and wanted to be involved." Brodie shrugged. "So I do what I do, you know?"

"My dad was the opposite. I would be the star player, or I would die trying."

Brodie's smile was everything. "I'm sure he's proud."

Even though Brodie watched the road and couldn't see him, Cato shrugged. "I wouldn't know. He's serving twenty-five to life for trying to kill my twin."

"Whoa."

"Yeah. I know. Sorry for saying too much." Cato had a bad habit of oversharing.

Brodie laughed and shot a quick glance Cato's way. "Nah. That whoa wasn't about your dad. It's because there's two of you. That's hot."

A surprised laugh burst from Cato. "Don't get too excited. We look nothing alike, and he's married to Jay Ames."

"Yeah. Messing with him would be a death sentence," Brodie said with a laugh.

Cato couldn't stop staring at Brodie. He was either gay or bi. Either way, Cato's interest doubled. He suddenly looked forward to this summer more than he ever expected.

Brodie lied when he acted as if he knew nothing about Cato's personal life. When Kieran had asked this favor of him, Brodie had looked into him. Plus, like everyone else in the world, he had seen the news of the toughest and most obnoxious defenseman in the league marrying Cato's twin. To say people were surprised was definitely an understatement. As a gay man, that had been a proud day for him. Every hockey player who stepped from the closet gave hope to every player who hadn't. Brodie didn't even own a closet, metaphorically speaking. He would be damned if he pretended to be someone he wasn't.

He had been lucky as hell to have parents who were intelligent and well-traveled. They brooked no ignorance. Brodie could always be himself. In his experience, the more comfort he showed in his sexuality, the easier it was for people to accept. He didn't hide. People didn't feel deceived. The matter was moved past quickly, never to be thought about again. That was why he had thrown those comments in, subtly letting Cato know about him. It was best to get it out of the way.

There was one thing that hadn't escaped his notice, though. Cato hadn't reacted the way most new players did. He couldn't count the times he had heard, "*You're gay?*" in the most surprised and condescending manner possible. Cato hadn't done that. In fact, Brodie felt Cato's stare. It was heavy on Brodie's skin. He felt its heat. Cato Janssen was in the closet.

Brodie pulled into the arena and found his reserved space. "Welcome to your new home." He watched Cato eye the place. Obviously, Cato had been on the ice before for away games. Brodie recognized it was different, knowing this would be his new world. He realized this had to be hard for Cato. "You'll be happy here." Even Brodie heard the care in his softly spoken statement.

Cato turned his head. Their gazes met. Brodie thanked God for his dark glasses, hiding his thoughts. Cato's light blue eyes were amazing. His blond hair was a mess from the wind. Cato could wreck a person. Brodie wouldn't let it be him.

"Let's get you inside." Brodie stepped from the vehicle before he did anything dumb. He felt Cato on his heels. Brodie tried to ignore the feeling of being stalked. He moved his sunglasses to the top of his head as they headed inside. Brodie led Cato to the locker room and to the gear he had already set out for him. Brodie motioned toward it. "These are from the brands courting you. Feel free to try out both before making your decision. The ice is yours for the next few hours. I have some shit to do, but I'll come get you when I'm ready to lock up." Brodie turned to meet Cato's stare.

Cato had already removed his shirt.

To Brodie's shame, his gaze moved down Cato's body. Deep, cut lines and valleys of perfection were right there for Brodie's enjoyment. He wished he had left his sunglasses on his face just a few minutes longer. There was zero chance Cato didn't catch the lustful gawking.

His gaze snapped back to Cato's face.

Cato smirked.

Brodie's spine stiffened. "I'll leave you to it." He walked away, determined to hang on to his pride. Damned if he didn't hear a low chuckle behind him as he ran for his life. Fantastic.

CHAPTER TWO

BRODIE PIDDLED AROUND FOR three hours, blasting music and killing time. He honestly didn't have shit to do. Brodie simply wanted Cato to get in some ice time. Toward the middle of last season, he had noticed a decline in Cato's play. At twenty-three, the guy had way too many good years left in him for the problem to be any sort of slowdown. He had been playing distracted. His heart hadn't been in the game. Brodie didn't want that for his team. They needed the old Cato.

At the three-hour mark, Brodie headed for the ice. For a few minutes, he watched Cato hit puck after puck. Sweat dripped from his hair, proving just how hard he had been at it. Brodie released a loud whistle, calling time.

Cato turned. His bright smile proved how much Cato loved having skates on the ice. This was his happy place. That was good. It was Brodie's home too. Cato skated his way. "That was fast."

Brodie chuckled. "It's been three hours."

Confusion crossed Cato's features be-fore disappearing behind a smile. "I guess time really flies when you're having fun."

The fact that he dripped with sweat from the exertion, and still called the day fun, said a lot about Cato's stamina. Fuck. That was hot. "Hit the shower and I'll take care of your gear."

With a nod, Cato skated off the ice and passed Brodie his stick. While Brodie followed, Cato removed gear as he went. This time, Brodie was better prepared for the sight of Cato's bare skin. When they reached the locker room and Cato sat, taking off his skates, Brodie stared at nothing. Cato was already nude from the waist up. Brodie knew Cato would drop his pants soon just to feed his ego.

"I don't really know anyone here."

The statement brought Brodie's stare Cato's way.

Cato kept going. "Would you like to go for a drink?"

Cato never looked at Brodie as he posed the question. His muscles were tensed, as if braced for rejection. Despite his better judgment, Brodie's heart went out to him. Getting traded to a town where you didn't know a soul had to fucking suck.

"Yeah. Sure. I know a place."

He watched Cato's muscles relax. "Great." Cato stood and passed along his skates.

Brodie's gaze moved away again. "I'll get these sharpened for you."

"I'll get showered for you."

At Cato's choice of words, Brodie looked his way again. This time, he kept his gaze firmly locked on Cato's eyes. That wasn't a better choice. Brodie still kept his pride. "Cool." He walked away, refusing to get sucked down the black hole of another closeted player. Brodie had been there, done that, and had all the scars to prove it. Mentally and physically. This would be a drink and nothing more. That was that.

Cato couldn't get past the way Brodie had looked at him when he had taken off his shirt. He also couldn't forget the way Brodie seemed to immediately hate himself for it. Brodie wasn't as friendly on the way to the bar. Thankfully, the place wasn't far. Discomfort had set in.

Cato eyed the sign. "Puck Drop. Great lure this close to the arena."

Brodie slipped from the Jeep. "A lot of the players hang out here during the season."

Cato followed Brodie, enjoying the show. There was no way Brodie didn't feel his eyes on him. He couldn't help it. Cato truly didn't intend to start anything. They would travel together for—hopefully—years. It was never a good idea to mix business and pleasure. Cato was simply incapable of not looking at Brodie. Each time he stared at Brodie's body, he caught sight of another tattoo. They were all amazing.

Brodie glanced over his shoulder as he moved to open the bar's door. He busted Cato eyeing the spot above his ass where his shirt had lifted a hair.

Cato didn't hide his actions. "Sorry. You have some awesome ink. I was trying to get a better look."

Open relief filled Brodie's features. "Oh. There's an award-winning artist who used to do all the team's ink before he moved to Phoenix. People all around the world pay him big bucks for a single piece. Since he married a now-retired Phoenix player, I usually either get inked when we play Phoenix, or I use his old partner here at a local shop."

Cato turned shameless. "I'd love to get a closer look sometime." He purposely kept his voice neutral, trying to keep Brodie off balance.

Brodie shrugged and let go of the door. "Sure." He moved down the sidewalk a few feet, so they weren't blocking the entrance. To his surprise, Brodie whipped his shirt up and over his head.

With open permission to stare, Cato took it all in, including the pierced nipples. He wondered what else was pierced. "Fuck." From the bottom of his heart, Cato meant it. He hadn't meant for that singular word to sound so sexual, but it was too late. Cato circled him, eyeing the tattoos and Brodie's body. Equipment managers didn't require the muscle it took to play, but it still took muscle. Brodie's body was lithe and defined. Cato honestly didn't notice a single tattoo, even though Brodie was completely covered.

He cleared his throat. "Amazing."

"Thanks." Brodie pulled his shirt back on and headed back toward the door. "Come on. I'll buy the first round."

Cato recognized running when he saw it. It was usually him headed for the hills.

Brodie needed to be inside the badly lit bar where he could hide his erection. The way Cato had cursed at the sight of him had immediately gotten him hard. He swore he could already hear that curse in just that tone against his ear while they fucked. Cato was dangerous. Brodie didn't want it.

He headed straight for the bar.

A hand touched the small of his back. Brodie turned, ready to set some things straight. Daire Jernigan stood at his side.

A bright smile lit his face. "Daire! Hey." It wasn't that he was excited to see Daire. In fact, he wanted to kick his own ass for the over-the-top greeting. He was just relieved it hadn't been Cato touching him. Unfortunately, his overzealous relief had Daire eyeing him too closely in a way he didn't like. He didn't need that bullshit.

Daire was the Chuckers' goalie. Everyone adored him. Women. Men. Children. The elderly. It didn't matter. Daire was impossible to hate. Sometimes, Brodie was the only exception.

"You walked right by me when you came through the door. Is everything okay?"

Even though Daire had a thick Canadian accent that doubly stood out in Cajun country, he was soft-spoken. Sometimes he made Brodie wonder if he had ever yelled in his life. Yelling would at least show he cared about something.

"Sorry. I'm good. Guess I was just in my head." Speaking of which, Brodie glanced around for the problem. He stood at their backs, looking uncomfortable. Brodie's irritation melted away. His heart squeezed. Brodie motioned Cato's way. "I've just been showing Cato around the area."

Daire turned slightly. He brightened. "Cato, nice to meet you." He held his hand out for Cato to shake. "I didn't think I'd get the chance until training camp. I'm Daire."

Cato smiled and accepted Daire's hand-shake. "It's nice to meet you. You have an impressive record."

"So do you."

Pressure lifted from Brodie's shoulders now that Cato had a second person to hang with. Honestly, the way Cato acted meeting Daire surprised Brodie. With the way he had been eyeing Brodie like a side of beef, Cato didn't seem to even no-tice Daire. Everyone noticed Daire. He was big, dark, and classically handsome in every way. Dark blue eyes. Cleft in his chin. Daire appealed to everyone. Brodie let it go. He ordered a Coke and a beer while the two talked. Once he paid and tipped, Brodie handed the beer to Cato.

"First round, as promised."

Cato eyed the Coke in his hand. "Where's yours?"

Brodie sipped his refreshing nonalcoholic beverage and hummed. "I don't drink. Even if I did, I'm driving. I can't risk the safety of the Chuckers' upcoming star."

Another player appeared at Brodie's side. Gustav kissed Brodie's temple. "There's my favorite person."

Brodie flashed the huge Swede a smile. This time, it was genuine. Gustav was the typical Swedish male. Blond-haired, blue-eyed, tall, and gorgeous. He was also kind and Brodie adored him despite their past. "Hey, Gustav. How have you been?"

Gustav nodded. "Great. I see you've made a new friend." He turned Cato's way. "I'm Gustav. You're Cato, right?"

Cato nodded. They did that handshake that turned into a weird shoulder bump Brodie supposed was certain men's version of a hug without embracing.

They exchanged pleasantries.

Brodie focused on Daire. "How have you been, seriously?" Daire was definitely a man who hid everything behind a smile, but Brodie knew him. He didn't drink, and he smelled like whiskey.

Daire held his stare.

Brodie dipped his chin and looked away. "You know my number." He hated himself as soon as the words left his lips.

A bright and fake smile stretched Daire's lips. He slung an arm across Gustav's shoulders. "Let's return to our drinks. It benefits us all for Brodie to make Cato fall madly in love with him, so he plays his heart out for the team." Daire met Cato's stare. "Seriously, Brodie is amazing. You'll see when the season starts. You won't be able to live without him."

Cato nodded. His gaze slid Brodie's way. "I don't doubt it."

A chill ran down Brodie's spine. Cato Janssen was dangerous. Brodie would have to watch his heart.

CHAPTER THREE

COLD AIR CHILLED CATO'S face as he sped across the ice. Lap after lap, he skated as fast as he could. His legs ached. He couldn't stop. His intensity kicked up by the minute.

"Are you trying to hurt yourself?"

The shout snapped Cato's focus. He spotted Brodie leaned against the wall. They met twice a week. Brodie let him in and let him know when it was time to leave. He took care of Cato's gear. The one thing he didn't do was try to be Cato's friend.

Cato skated toward the wall. "Do you skate?"

"Of course." Brodie wasn't a smart-ass about it. Just matter of fact.

"Get your skates and join me."

Brodie eyed him. His expression remained unreadable. "Will you stop trying to kill yourself if I do?"

A smile snapped to Cato's lips. "I'll behave."

With a nod, Brodie disappeared. In no time, he was back and gliding out onto the ice. He moved with the confidence of a professional.

Cato skated backward, keeping pace with him. Nostalgia washed over him at the idea of simply skating for pleasure. "When my brother and I were kids, my dad would drop me at the rink and leave me all day, expecting me to spend hours perfecting every aspect of play. I always made him bring Callan too, but he wouldn't buy Callan skates because he was too much of a pansy." Cato used air quotes on the last words, mocking his father's hatred. "So I lied and said youth league required two pairs of skates. I would drag Callan onto the ice. He was such a graceful skater. I think—if anyone had invested half as much in him as they did me—he could've been a figure skater."

"You miss him."

Cato easily continued skating backward, keeping track of every turn. "I've never gone this long without him."

Brodie's expression never changed. He didn't judge Cato. "Is that why you're killing yourself? You're upset?"

Cato didn't lie. "I'm not upset. I'm bitter."

"For being traded?"

Cato snorted. "About everything. For the life of me, I'll never understand how I can love something so much while it steals everything good from me." He had no idea why he said the things he did. Maybe he had kept them bottled too long. Possibly Brodie just had one of those faces. Most likely, Brodie was right. Cato was killing himself.

For a moment, Brodie stared at him, as if weighing his words. "If I ask you something, will you be honest with me?"

Cato shrugged. They skated in circles, facing each other. It was an oddly intimate moment. "I've already confessed more to you than I have anyone else in ages."

"Don't kick my ass."

Cato chuckled. That was such an odd thing to say. "Why would I kick your ass?"

"Are you gay?"

Cato's smile slipped away. Not once in his twenty-three years had he put a label on himself. While he had admitted to being in love with his brother's husband, he had never used the word gay when talking about himself. Maybe that would make it real.

"I promise anything said today won't leave here."

Cato stopped skating.

Brodie did too.

They held each other's stare. "Yeah. I'm gay." Fuck. He didn't know how he expected he would feel. It wasn't freeing.

Brodie stared at him. He didn't say a word.

Cato's nervousness stole his tongue and ran. "I know what you're thinking. You want to tell me it doesn't matter. That people won't care, but it does, and they do."

"I know."

Cato started slowly skating backward again. Brodie kept pace with him. Their gazes never wavered.

"Which mascot do you think would beat you in a cage match?"

A loud bark of laughter burst from Cato at the question. As far as subject changes went, it worked. Cato considered the question. "Majors, minors, or both?"

"Majors."

"New York," Cato said immediately.

A bright smile snapped to Brodie's lips. "Only because he'd fight dirty."

"God, they fight so dirty there," Cato said in full agreement.

They shared a smile. Cato didn't feel so alone.

Fuck. Cato's eyes broke him. There was something different about him. Brodie couldn't explain it. He tormented himself, as if terrified of being seen as having the tiniest imperfection. Brodie ached for him. He couldn't imagine the pressure and loneliness of Cato's current position. He enjoyed making Cato smile.

"Likely all the mascots could take me, except Des Moines. I think I could take that dude."

A loud snort burst from Cato. "I actually think their mascot is a girl."

Brodie thought about it. "Never mind, then. She could probably take me."

Cato nodded. "Women don't fight fair."

They shared another laugh. For a moment, they held each other's stare. Cato's eyes shone bright with happiness—in a way they hadn't since they'd met. Brodie's skin heated. He had done that. Brodie was the reason Cato smiled. He didn't know why that caused butterflies to stir in his stomach, but it did.

"But do you think you could beat her in a foot race?"

Brodie scoffed at the question. "Dude, I would smoke her ass in a foot race."

Cato's sexy-sounding chuckle was everything. Brodie couldn't stop smiling. Unexpectedly, Cato grabbed his hands and started speed-skating backward, around the ice. A laugh ripped from Brodie. Cato was stupidly talented. He didn't even look, and he still easily maneuvered around everything like he had the ice memorized. Likely, he did. The moment reminded Brodie of how skating could be just for fun. Since Cato probably needed the reminder too, Brodie didn't pull away. Brodie roared with laughter as Cato snatched him off his feet and started spinning. By the time Cato stopped, Brodie's head was a dizzy mess. Cato wasn't even winded.

Cato set Brodie on his feet but didn't release him. Brodie realized he clung to Cato's wide chest. He skated back a hair, putting space between them.

A sweet smile touched Cato's lips. "Thank you. I needed that."

Damn. Brodie's heart was in trouble. He didn't know how to stop. "Anytime."

"I'll take you up on that."

Brodie looked away. He couldn't hold Cato's stare any longer. "I should let you change. It's about time to lock up."

"Okay."

Neither of them moved.

Brodie gathered his strength and met Cato's stare again. If he had turned his head and seen hunger in Cato's eyes, Brodie would have been fine. He was used to people wanting to fuck and nothing more. Brodie didn't know what he saw in Cato's expression, but it scared the shit out of him. Some things a person could survive. Cato likely wasn't on that list.

Chapter Four

BRODIE NEEDED THE BREAK from Cato. He had been meeting Cato every Tuesday and Thursday for six weeks. Those precious four days between Thursday and Tuesday always saved his sanity. He needed ink therapy. Brodie sat inside Masked Image, getting his sleeve tattoos extended down his hands. He was only doing one today. Tommy, the second greatest tattoo artist on the planet—as far as Brodie was concerned anyway—was hard as hell to book these days. He already had two more customers coming after him, so Brodie couldn't do both. Brodie would take what he could get and set up another appointment for the other. With the needle moving across his skin, Brodie's mind blanked. The pain grounded him. He didn't think about Cato at all. His brain was tired of obsessing about the sexy guy who had stormed into his life.

The door opened, spilling in the sunlight. Cato stepped through the door with Daire. They both were all smiles and chatting. Then they looked Brodie's way.

"Holy hell. It's Brodie," Daire called, making Brodie smile despite himself.

Brodie's gaze moved between them. "Hey. Are you two getting inked today?"

Cato shook his head. "Not me. Just Daire. We were already out, so I tagged along to meet this amazing artist everyone's been telling me about."

Tommy chuckled.

Brodie looked his way and winked. "You know we love you."

The jet-black hair that mostly hid his face bobbed as Tommy nodded. He looked up from his task and met Brodie's stare for half a second. His eerily light green eyes always held Brodie slightly captivated. "The feeling is mutual, man." Tommy cleaned off his hand before coating it in his special brand of ointment and covering it. "You know how to care for it."

Brodie nodded and moved from the chair. He had already paid, adding a tip, so he was free to go. Instead, he moved to a different chair, the only one was knee to knee with Cato. If he ran off, Daire would call him on it. That was who he was. Daire knew him too well. Brodie also knew Daire. He was curious as hell what the two were doing together, but he wouldn't ask.

"What are you getting done today?"

Daire peeled off his shirt. Brodie forcefully kept his gaze locked on Daire's face. He already knew Daire had an amazing body. "I'm getting my back piece finished." He turned, showing off a huge phoenix that was nearly complete.

Brodie nodded. "It's looking good."

"What do you have planned after this?"

Brodie shrugged at Daire's question. "I'm supposed to meet Kieran and Henley for dinner."

"Me too," Cato said, bringing Brodie's gaze his way.

"Oh." That was all Brodie had. Kieran hadn't mentioned anyone else would be joining them.

Daire spoke up. "This will take a while. If Brodie is willing, you should go with him, so you're not late to dinner."

There was absolutely nothing backing his thoughts, but Brodie felt like he had been set up. It didn't matter he knew it wasn't true.

"I don't want to put Brodie out. I'll just call an Uber."

Fuck. "It's fine. You can ride with me." He was really tempted to ask how Cato intended to leave here on time to begin with. Damn.

They spent another half an hour chatting. Cato's knee kept bumping his. More than once, Brodie realized he leaned Cato's way. He had to force himself to hold his space. Finally, he checked his watch.

"We'd better head out. Are you ready?"

Cato's light blue gaze moved his way. The muscles in Brodie's stomach clenched as Cato's gaze dropped to Brodie's lips before moving back to meet his stare. "Sure. I'm ready whenever you are."

Brodie swore Cato's words had a double meaning. He looked away and stood. Brodie nodded Tommy's way. "See you next weekend, same time."

Tommy nodded. He lifted his chin, exposing his face more than usual. His lip ring caught the light as he smiled. "See you, man."

He was honestly super-hot in a punk sort of way. Brodie had never understood why the guy went out of his way to hide himself.

They said their goodbyes and headed for Brodie's Jeep. He realized how close they walked when their arms bumped. Brodie shook his head. He had no clue what was happening here.

Seeing Kieran and Henley together outside a work setting warmed Cato's heart. In his playing days, Henley had been a hardcore badass. It was nice to see him so openly loving his husband. Not that Cato imagined it was hard. Kieran had light blond hair that captured the light and the scariest gray eyes Cato had ever seen. Not only was he beautiful, but he also went out of his way to ensure the world knew Henley was his everything. They held hands. Kieran opened every door for him. He always ensured Henley went first in every situation. Cato couldn't stop studying every aspect of them. He desperately wanted to ask how Henley had handled the pressure of being out and proud in their sport. The words stuck in his throat.

"Have either of you ever heard of the show *Spectral Investigations*?" The question caught Cato off guard with his head in the clouds.

"No," Cato said at the same time Brodie said, "Yes."

Kieran chuckled. He looked more relaxed tonight than Cato had ever seen him. Kieran actually wore jeans and a T-shirt. The outfit looked wrong on him. He seemed too human.

"It's a popular show on cable TV where a group of paranormal investigators travel the country, exploring haunted locations."

Cato nodded. That would explain why he had never heard of it. He didn't watch that bullshit.

Kieran kept going at Cato's nod. "They're currently filming their upcoming season. This year, at each location, they're inviting local celebrities to investigate with them."

"That sounds like a blast," Brodie said, sounding genuinely excited.

"I'm glad you feel that way," Kieran said, switching his gaze between them. "Since I represent you both, and the Chuckers belong to the entire state of Louisiana—not just New Orleans—I pitched for you two to be on the show."

Cato's eyebrows rose.

Brodie leaned forward, obviously loving the idea. "Seriously?"

Kieran nodded. "They're investigating the Smythe Hotel in Shreveport this weekend. It's supposed to be the most haunted hotel in the world. The show has booked you both flights and you'll actually be staying in the hotel. You'll spend three days investigating with their team. Congratulations."

"Holy shit. That's awesome. I freaking love that show. I can't wait to meet all the guys."

Cato didn't care about the show. While he imagined it would likely be a good time, and it was definitely something different, he was thrilled at the idea of spending three days with Brodie. Three days where he couldn't run.

"That's amazing," Cato said before anyone thought he was ungrateful.

Brodie looked his way. His eyes were alight with happiness. "I've always wanted to do this. We'll have so much fun. Fuck. I'll have to cancel my next appointment with Tommy. It's okay, though. We get to be on my favorite show."

Damn, he was gorgeous. "I can't wait." Seriously. Cato meant it. He didn't believe in ghosts. That didn't matter. Brodie looked happy. Cato wanted to keep him that way. For a moment, they simply stared at each other. The air changed. A knot formed in Cato's stomach. He seriously didn't know what it was about the guy. Cato couldn't stop himself from sneaking a peek at Brodie's lips. They were perfect. His stomach growled. Brodie looked away. Cato forced his attention back Kieran's way. Kieran lifted Henley's hand and pressed the back of it to his lips while he held Cato's stare. A sweet smile softened Henley's face. A pang of jealousy hit Cato. He so badly wanted what they had. He had a bad feeling Kieran knew it, and it would never happen.

Cato dropped his gaze to the menu, focusing on what he could have: an expensive meal. God knew he had money, thanks to Kieran. Yep. Lots of money that kept growing. He didn't have to worry about a thing, except the pains in his chest. Bitterness rose inside him. He clenched his fists beneath the table. His eyes burned. Frustration nearly broke him.

Brodie touched his thigh, capturing Cato's attention. Cato looked his way. "Are you okay?"

The air cleared with Brodie's hand on his thigh. He never got human contact anymore. No one touched him. Cato nodded. "I'm good."

Brodie eyed him for a moment. Finally, he nodded. "Okay." He squeezed Cato's thigh once before pulling away. Cato wanted to beg Brodie to touch him again. He lifted his chin. His gaze collided with Kieran's eerie gray eyes again. For a moment, he swore Kieran knew exactly what he had been thinking. Cato went back to the menu. He couldn't let anyone see him. If they did, he might break.

CHAPTER FIVE

THE FLIGHT TO SHREVEPORT was a quick one. In no time, they were in a cab and headed to the hotel. Brodie couldn't stop chatting about everything and nothing. He was nervous. Poor Cato was probably ready to stuff a sock in his mouth. He hadn't shown an ounce of impatience. In fact, he had held Brodie's stare and seemed to hang on every word. For real, he was a trooper.

As they pulled up to the hotel, Brodie leaned closer to the window and eyed the building. It was massive and creepy. Even though the place probably only looked that way because it was old and Brodie had heard the horror stories, he was still uneasy. Cato looked absolutely unfazed. Of course, he had admitted to not believing in ghosts. He likely expected nothing would happen this weekend.

They grabbed their bags and headed inside. Brodie's head turned in every direction, taking it all in. The walls and high ceiling were all painted with murals. Some of the faces, peeking through the painted nonsense, were downright terrifying. Cato strolled right up to the front desk without checking out a thing. Of course, they practically lived in hotels six months out of the year. As a nonbeliever, this probably felt like just another night away from home to him.

Brodie hung back, expecting to check in next. To his surprise, the woman circled the counter and greeted them. "Hey, guys. Welcome to the famous Smythe Hotel. I'm Candace. The team has requested I take you on a quick tour before I show you to your room. We'll hit the highlights, since the place is too big to see in only a few minutes. But if you have questions, feel free to ask."

Even though he hadn't expected the over-the-top greeting, he gladly passed his bags along to the bellhop. He was ready to see everything. They followed on the blonde's heels.

"The hotel was built in nineteen twenty by a wealthy banker, George Smythe.

As you might know, during that time, there was a clash of cultures between modernization and those who believed strongly people should turn to religion instead of material things. Smythe was a forward-thinking man. The more zealots pushed, the more the hotel grew. He hired the best artists in the world to create murals around the building. A movie theater was built, drawing wealthy guests from all over the country."

She opened a set of doors leading into a theater that had obviously been preserved over the years. Brodie imagined it still looked the way it had in its glory days.

"Do they still show movies here?" Cato asked, seeming surprisingly interested.

"They do, but only on Halloween. It's a double feature of *Nosferatu* and *Dr. Jekyll and Mr. Hyde*."

"Sounds fun."

She smiled at Cato. Her gaze made a subtle sweep of his body. An inner sigh rang through Brodie's head. He hoped he didn't have to witness too much flirting. Sometimes it sucked being around so many muscular and famous men.

She moved on. "This is one of our more active areas. In nineteen thirty-two, during the Great Depression, like everything, the hotel struggled. Mr. Smythe held on through what most suspect were nefarious means as many high-profile members of the mafia were often seen at the hotel. That's what led to one of the most notorious mass shootings in history. Obviously, that wasn't really a term back then, but that's what it was. The theater was rented out for the day for a special showing for Pip 'three fingers' Antonelli's birthday. I guess having that many rival members in once place was too much temptation. Shorty Hamilton and his men showed up fifteen minutes in, slaughtering twenty-three people in under five minutes right where you're standing."

Brodie was invested. "What sort of things happen in this room?"

"Voices. Doors slamming. People see shadows move across the screen."

Cato stayed blank-faced.

Brodie couldn't wait to get started.

"Moving on." She waved them along and headed for the elevator. "Some people believe this hotel is cursed. Several deaths have been documented here, and many more are believed to have gone unreported. There's a rumor someone was decapitated by this very elevator, trying to climb out while it was stuck. That's never been substantiated."

They stepped off the elevator. "However, we do have several records of suicides here." She unlocked a hotel room door. "And this is where a man murdered his family before taking his own life. Not only is it the most haunted room in the hotel, but it's also where you two will be staying."

They two. In one room. There was one bed. It wasn't even a big bed. They exchanged a look.

Brodie broke first. "Would it be possible for me to get another room? This doesn't really look big enough for both of us."

She laughed. When no one else did, her laughter died. "It's Cajun Fire Music Festival week. You won't find an empty room anywhere in town. The only reason you have this one is because we don't rent it out. No one has ever made it through the night without wanting a refund. Finally, we had to throw in the towel and stop allowing people to sleep here."

Cato and Brodie shared another look. Neither of them said it, but Brodie knew they had the same thought. Ghosts were the last thing they had to fear from this situation.

Despite his opinion on ghosts, Cato was having a great time. Brodie looked happy and hadn't stopped talking all day. The team turned out to be a group of four guys who all seemed amazing. After introductions and a rundown of how the weekend would go, they had been split into teams. Brodie had been paired with a giant teddy bear-looking guy named Jim. Cato had gotten the self-proclaimed tech nerd of the group, Hugh. Hugh was five foot four if he was an inch, but he entered every room with a confidence Cato admired.

While the hotel was fully booked, certain areas of the hotel had been reserved for the show. The theater, dining hall, and a part of the building currently under construction were all quiet zones for filming. They waited until the middle of the night to get started when there would be even less chance of any noise interference. Cato and Hugh covered the theater. A cameraman followed their every move while the room was also covered in cameras to catch every detail from every angle.

Hugh and Cato chose seats in the theater and sat in the dark. "I hear you don't believe in the paranormal."

Cato smiled at the comment. "I wouldn't say I'm a nonbeliever as much as a skeptic. Since nothing remotely paranormal has ever happened to me, it sounds a bit wild to me when people claim to have seen things."

Hugh nodded. He kept his gaze moving, as if he didn't want to miss a thing. "People say they hear voices in here. What do you say we do a little call and response?"

Cato shrugged. "I'm game."

Hugh pulled out a small device. "This is an EVP recorder. It picks up sounds not discernible to the human ear. So, in theory, when I ask questions, any spirits in the room can speak into the device. When we play back the recording, we should be able to hear their response."

"Okay."

Hugh started the device. "Is there anyone with us tonight?" He paused before asking the next question. Cato assumed it was to give the ghosts time to answer. "Are you angry about your death?" Another pause. "Can you tell us your name?"

He stopped the recorder. "Let's see if we caught anything."

Hugh rewound the device.

Cato leaned closer to listen.

"Is there anyone with us tonight?" No response. "Are you angry about your death?"

Cato jumped when a growled, almost demonic-sounding voice answered, "Yes."

They cast each other a shocked look.

Hugh stopped the recording. "Is it just me, or did that voice sound demonic?"

Cato shook his head. "It definitely sounded angry."

A crash sounded across the theater. They jumped to their feet.

"What the hell was that?" Hugh took off toward the sound. "What the fuck, man? Is that one of the cameras?" Hugh picked up the camera that had smashed to the ground. He looked Cato's way. "Dude, you saw me hang this camera. It was bolted in place with trail cam straps. There's no way it could just fall."

Cato didn't know what to say. He had to agree. It shouldn't have fallen. Something moved in the corner of Cato's vision. He spun. "Did you see that?"

Hugh eyed the spot where something had definitely moved. "I did, but I don't know what it was. It was almost like a shadow peeked out and then disappeared again." Hugh grabbed his handheld radio. "Cameron."

"What's up, buddy?"

"Can you pull up the camera footage in the theater and see if we caught anything? We have shit happening all around us in here."

Static came through the radio for a second. "Sure thing."

Cato had no idea what was happening. He didn't know what would be on that footage. Oddly, all Cato knew was he was having a blast.

Chapter Six

BRODIE HAD GOTTEN PAIRED with a guy named Jim for the weekend. Jim was every bit of two hundred and fifty pounds, with a beard and beefy arms. He was incredibly sweet, and Brodie was fucking terrified. Whereas the hotel was simply creepy during the day, it was downright horrible at night. The place had a vibe. He kept expecting someone would jump out at any moment.

"From what we found in our research, this dining hall is where a waiter was stabbed to death in the sixties. Apparently, he had been having an affair with a married coworker. One night, her husband confronted the guy and stabbed him repeatedly in front of dozens of witnesses."

"That's crazy."

Jim nodded. "But not unjustified."

"Agreed," Brodie said, thankful he hadn't been the one to say it first.

Jim held up a wooden box with dials and a speaker. "This is a ghost box." Brodie knew what it was, but they had warned him the guys would have to explain each piece of equipment for any new viewers. "It's picks up radio waves in different frequencies. In theory, ghosts can use those waves to speak, and the radio should spit out the sound."

Brodie nodded. "Sounds great. Let's ask some questions."

A smile snapped to Jim's lips at Brodie's enthusiasm. "Let's get it." He turned one dial and loud static filled the air. "Is there anyone here with us?"

The static got louder for a second. "Yes."

Brodie wanted to dance in place in his excitement. He couldn't help but ask a question too. "Is this the waiter who was murdered here by a jealous husband?"

Static.

"Is this someone else?" Jim asked loudly.

"Yes."

Jim carried the box around as if looking for the best signal. "If you're not the waiter, who are you?"

"Leave."

"You want us to leave?" Brodie asked for clarification.

"Die."

Jim's forehead furrowed. "Are you saying we'll die if we don't leave?"

"Demon."

They exchanged a look. "Did they just say demon?"

Brodie nodded.

"In the theater."

Brodie's heart sped. "There's a demon in the theater?"

"Yes."

They held each other's stare. Jim shook his head. "Dude, who's covering the theater?"

Brodie had no idea. They had been given their assignment first and immediately got started. He shrugged and shook his head.

Jim switched off the box and pulled his handheld radio from his belt. "Hey, guys."

A voice came through the radio. "What's up?"

"Who's covering the theater?"

"Hugh and Cato. Why?"

Brodie's pulse pounded in his ears. He needed Cato to be okay.

"Tell them to be careful. We just got a voice through the ghost box saying there's a demon in the theater."

"A demon?"

"That's what it said, man."

A door slammed at their backs. Everyone jumped, including the cameraman. A startled curse flew from Brodie's lips. It looked like they were in for a long night.

By the time they called it a night, Cato was exhausted. Between the bursts of adrenaline and being up all night, he didn't think even a ghost could disturb his sleep. Brodie looked every bit as exhausted. They reached the room at the same time.

"You can have the shower first, if you want," Cato offered. All he wanted was to sit for a moment.

Brodie nodded. "Thanks. Did y'all see anything?"

"Too much."

To his surprise, Brodie didn't gloat. "Yeah, us too. This place is wild."

Cato plopped down on a wooden chair by the bed. "It's definitely that." He watched Brodie gather his things and head into the bathroom. The water fired to life. Cato pulled out his phone, ready to play games to kill time. The battery was dead. He plugged up the device and went back to staring at nothing. Every few seconds, he would turn his head when he swore something moved. The entire night had him fucked in the head.

Brodie stepped from the bathroom in nothing but shorts. Cato forgot everything. "Are the nipple piercings the only ones you have?"

Brodie smirked.

Cato shook his head and headed inside the bathroom. The mirror was already fogged up and steam hung in the air. Somehow, the bathroom seemed even creepier than the bedroom. He brushed his teeth and showered in record time before pulling on a pair of shorts. With water still streaming down his skin, he killed the light and headed out. He found Brodie tucked beneath the covers.

"I can sleep in the chair if you want."

Brodie snorted. "Don't be ridiculous. There's no reason we can't share the bed. Plus, I'm so damn tired, I probably won't even notice you."

"Same." Cato turned off the lights and climbed in next to Brodie. On his back, he stared at the ceiling. A huge part of him was hyper aware of Brodie's shoulder against his. Another part of him couldn't stop checking the shadows. This whole ordeal had made him ridiculously paranoid. Minutes ticked by. He swore it felt like someone tugged on the covers. Cato told himself it was just Brodie moving, even though he hadn't felt Brodie move. It happened again.

"I can't sleep."

A smile snapped to Cato's lips. He turned his head. Brodie rolled onto his side. His eyes glistened in the dark from the light coming through the window.

"I can't either."

They stared at each other. Each breath Cato took came harder than the last. The air between them thickened. His heart raced. Cato knew something would happen. He just didn't know what. In a flash, Brodie's body covered his. Their mouths clashed. He couldn't say which of them made the first move. It didn't matter. Their hands were everywhere while their tongues battled. Cato shoved his hands down the back of Brodie's shorts. He squeezed the ass cheeks that had been driving him crazy for weeks. Brodie kissed like a man who loved it. Like a man with a practiced mouth. Cato's dick wept and strained against the waistband of his shorts. He controlled the lower half of Brodie's body, rocking Brodie against him. His hips lifted, grinding his erection against Brodie. Cato didn't think about the consequences or tomorrow. He didn't care about anything but the moment.

Brodie bit his bottom lip.

Cato groaned. "Fuck, Brodie." He couldn't recall ever being this turned on. He had to know. Cato shoved his hand between them and stroked Brodie's dick, hunting for piercings. He wasn't disappointed. Brodie had a king's crown. Damn, that was hot.

Brodie sat back on his heels and set Cato's erection free. They held each other's stare as they pleasured each other. Cato understood this was as far as things would go. If they stopped to hunt down lube and condoms, they would come to their senses. Cato didn't want the moment to end. Brodie had no idea what he gave Cato. Cato had been hurting and struggling to keep going. Brodie's touch was hope.

"You're so incredibly sexy." Cato had to let Brodie know he was wanted. "I've pictured you just like this."

"Same. Come for me."

Cato focused on the hand on his cock. He savored the sensation and matched Brodie's pace. Brodie shot cum onto Cato's chest. The sexy moment pushed Cato over the edge. His body shook as he gasped for air and his cum joined Brodic's.

Brodie fell forward and claimed Cato's mouth. Their tongues played as their breathing slowed. Then Brodie said the words that elated and broke him all at once.

"I won't tell."

Chapter Seven

Cato didn't hear from Brodie until the next Thursday, causing him to miss his Tuesday training. Even then, he only texted Cato could come and then he left the building unlocked. Cato didn't set eyes on him. Throughout their weekend together, each time they went to bed, they had touched each other through the night. It hadn't gone beyond touching. Now that they were home, it seemed

Brodie was done. Cato wasn't, but he couldn't make Brodie see him.

Next week, the entire team would be back on the ice, readying for the season. This was his last chance to have Brodie alone. Cato couldn't bring himself to go as hard. Thoughts of Brodie plagued his mind. He honestly didn't know what was happening between them. Maybe nothing. Still, Cato wanted more.

By the time Cato skated off the ice, giving up for the day, he was ready to give up in every way. His mind had been such a fucking mess since before he moved to New Orleans. It was exhausting being him. He sat on a bench in the locker room and took off his skates. After setting them aside, he simply sat there. He didn't hear or see anything. Cato disconnected.

Then he blinked and Brodie stood between his knees.

With his chin tilted up, Cato stared at Brodie. He didn't speak. Brodie eased Cato's shirt up and over his head. Cato let him have it. When Brodie's hands touched his bare shoulders, Cato ran his hands up the backs of Brodie's thighs until he could squeeze his ass. Still, they didn't speak or look away.

Cato's hands moved to Brodie's hips. He followed Brodie's waistband around until he reached the button on his jeans. Cato popped it open. He slid down the zipper. They never broke eye contact. Cato leaned in and licked the piercing he loved so much. A shaky-sounding breath escaped Brodie.

"I want you inside me."

Goosebumps rose on Cato's skin. He had never heard anything hotter just because it came from Brodie. Still. "I need you to be sure. I don't want you to regret me."

Brodie took Cato's hand and turned away. Cato followed without question. He led Cato into an office he had never seen, but it had Brodie's name on the door. Cato closed the door behind them. Brodie picked up a condom and lube from the desk, proving he had been pre-pared for this offer.

Cato held his stare as he set his cock free. Brodie pushed his pants down. His serious expression proved how much thought he had put into this move. He wouldn't regret Cato.

Cato suited up and coated the outside of the condom with lube. That was where he lost his patience. His mouth slammed against Brodie's. Cato snatched Brodie off his feet. Brodie braced himself on the edge of the desk. Cato recognized he had skipped several steps of foreplay, but he was half crazed. He was one hundred percent sure he would die if he didn't get inside Brodie. Cato impaled him.

Brodie's head fell back. He moaned. It sounded like it came from the soul.

God, he was amazing, beautiful, and responsive. Cato had never felt the way Brodie made him feel. No one had ever so openly desired him without shame. He couldn't look away from Brodie's face.

Cato stroked Brodie's sexy pierced cock as he thrust. Brodie sucked air. Cato did too. Brodie's asshole felt amazing. That was not what fucked with him the most.

It was Brodie. Cato couldn't stop taking in every detail of his open lust. It was for him. Cato's balls drew up tight. He wasn't ready. Pressure climbed his shaft. Cato's heart broke at the idea of their moment being done. He didn't want to return to the confusion, questioning if Brodie would be hot or cold today. Cato wanted to stay like this.

His body didn't give him a choice. Cato thrust faster and harder. Need overtook every other emotion. He was greedy for Brodie's ass. Cato had to pound it. Brodie's cries turned desperate. Cato had to please him. He couldn't stop doing the things that brought them closer to blowing. Brodie made a sound that Cato knew would burn into his memories. His body clenched and his cock spit.

A stuttered cry ripped from Cato. The pressure transformed into ecstasy. He rocked inside Brodie, savoring those final pumps of pleasure. His breathing sounded ragged as he buried himself deep one final time. He shook as he held Brodie tightly against his chest. His lips sought any place they could reach. Even with every drop of his cum stolen from him, Cato hadn't had enough. He needed more from Brodie.

"Have dinner with me."

Brodie's soft lips whisked his neck. "Okay."

Cato's eyes fell closed. He was in heaven.

Everything about Cato surprised Brodie, and never in a bad way. It was an odd hour for dinner. Even though it was way too late for lunch, it felt way too early for dinner. The restaurant Cato chose was nearly empty. Maybe that was why Cato didn't hesitate to slide into the same side of the booth as him. Whatever the reason, Brodie's heart was a mess.

Cato played with his thigh, just out of sight. He didn't seem the least bit concerned about being seen with him in public. For someone who had barely survived being hidden by a different hockey player, it felt fucking amazing. He had Brodie's heart's attention. It was terrifying.

Before leaving for dinner, they had showered together. It had been leisurely and sexy as hell. Cato had watched him with something in his gaze Brodie couldn't voice. Now they ate and talked. He swore he had never felt so comfortable with anyone's company.

"Is it crazy that I'd love to go on another ghost hunt?"

Brodie laughed at the guilt in Cato's expression. "Not as far as I'm concerned. That was a fucking blast." Cato's equal excitement had him digging into the discussion. "I go to this convention every year for like scary movies, paranormal shows, and things of that nature. It's in October, if you're interested in going with me this year. Anyhow, since my first year, they've been sending me emails from this one paranormal team. You can buy tickets to join them on various investigations around the country. I've thought about doing it a hundred times, but I don't want to go alone."

Cato didn't even hesitate. "Let's do it."

Brodie practically bounced in his seat. No one ever nerded out with him on the things that interested him. "I'll find the latest email and send it to you. We can compare it to the season's schedule and find something that works."

Cato's light blue eyes seemed even lighter when he was openly happy.

The guilt was back in Cato's expression. "I hate to admit it, but I was dreading this season. As much as I love the ice beneath my skates, California was my home, you know? It's where my twin is. Where my friends are. Now all those friends will be my opponents. I resented this trade more than I can vocalize."

Brodie wasn't surprised. He would feel the same way if he suddenly found himself two thousand miles from home with another team.

Cato's expression changed as he continued. A slight smile touched his lips. "But now, I can't wait to be trapped on the road with you."

Goddamn. There was no way Cato could understand. He said all the right things and meant them. Cato was too easy to read to lie.

Brodie's gaze moved over Cato's face, soaking up a moment of being the center of attention. "Same."

They shared a smile. Something grew larger between them. It was the blooming of something new and beautiful. Brodie had spent days thinking about this from every angle before making his move today. His mind was set. He would nurture this and hope for the best. Cato certainly couldn't destroy him any more than Daire already had.

Chapter Eight

A LAUGH BURBLED IN Cato's throat as he sped across the ice. He passed the puck. It came flying back his way just as fast. The small black disc that meant everything got trapped against the wall. Jay's body slammed against him, bashing him against the glass.

"It's good to see you, brother."

Cato ignored him as he fought for the puck. He had honestly thought he would feel torn the first time he played his old team. Cato didn't. His competitive nature refused to let him lose. No matter the opponent. Cato knocked the puck loose. Gustav retrieved it. In seconds, the score horn blasted, making the crowd roar. Cato couldn't stop smiling. He was back. Brodie watched from somewhere in the arena. His brother was in town. Everything felt right in his world. By the time the buzzer sounded, declaring them the winner, sweat coated every inch of Cato's skin. Adrenaline pumped through his veins. He needed a shower and to fuck. The latter part would be awhile. They had plans and company tonight.

Cato made his way to the locker room. They celebrated between the coach's speech and showers. Cato's impatience hit an all-time high by the time the locker room cleared. He wouldn't leave until Brodie did.

Brodie moved around the locker room, gathering gear. Once he had things separated and ready for him to focus on tomorrow, they would leave. Brodie couldn't take off before then. Cato was fine to wait. He was honestly a little nervous about tonight.

It was Halloween. Their episode on *Spectral Investigations* aired tonight. They planned to do a group watch with some of the team, Cato's twin and brother-in-law. Cato didn't plan to hide Brodie. He didn't know how it would go.

The thing was, they had been exclusive for four months, since the show had been recorded. In those months, Cato had made a huge discovery. One he should have realized earlier, since it had been the same for Callan and Jay. Even though they were a couple, and did nothing to hide it, people seemed either ludicrously oblivious or simply didn't care. It was almost a don't ask don't tell situation. But tonight, Cato knew his twin wouldn't play dumb. Not to mention Jay would be there. They hadn't seen each other since the wedding. Since Cato had admitted to being in love with Jay just hours before he married Cato's twin. Things felt awkward between them. Like that greeting on the ice, it was as if Jay couldn't stop calling him brother, reminding Cato of his place. Cato didn't know how he would feel when they were face to face again. He was scared as hell nothing had changed and that would change everything between Brodie and him.

Brodie appeared from nowhere. His arms encircled Cato's neck from behind. Cato stayed seated on the bench and savored the sensation of Brodie holding him. Brodie kissed the shell of his ear. Cato closed his eyes and focused on the way Brodie's soft lips felt against his skin. His entire body was on high alert. No part of him was left unaffected.

"Mhmm. There he is."

Brodie chuckled against his ear. "You looked incredible out there tonight. I'm proud of you."

Cato swore his chest swelled to twice the size. "You make me better."

He felt Brodie's lips shape into a smile against his ear. Still, he argued. "Don't do that. It's your hard work. Your talent."

"Your support," Cato added.

Brodie squeezed him. "Are you ready to see yourself on TV in a different setting?"

Cato laughed. "Not really. I'm sure I did at least one horrifyingly embarrassing thing. If so, these guys will never let me live it down."

With a laugh, Brodie stepped away. "Come on. We'll know soon enough."

Cato stood and turned. He caught sight of Brodie's expression and his heart sped. Sometimes, he would catch Brodie at just the right moment. Those brief glimpses always left him wondering if Brodie felt as much for him as Cato felt for him. He was too scared to ask. It didn't help he didn't understand his feelings. Cato had never felt this way before. He hoped like hell he didn't fuck it up.

Brodie had intentionally moved a little slower tonight. While he had sneaked into Cato's room during every travel game, and they left together after every home game, no one had seen them quite like they would tonight. Not to mention Cato's twin was in town. It felt like he was being taken to meet the family. Tonight felt like a big deal—like they would cross an invisible line in the sand.

They had ridden to the arena together, the way they always did these days. As Cato's home came into view, Brodie's nerves stretched to the limit. Cars already sat in the driveway. Cato had to maneuver around one to get inside the garage where Brodie's Jeep already sat. In that moment, it hit Brodie exactly how entwined their lives had become.

As they came through the door, they found Daire eating chips and trading barbs with Jay. A smaller man with the most beautiful features Brodie had ever seen lit from the inside at the sight of them. He ran at Cato. Cato snatched him from his feet.

"Holy shit. I've missed you."

Jay ran their way, mimicking the blond in Cato's arms. He pretended as if he, too, planned to jump into Cato's arms. "It's my brother!"

Cato laughed. "Hey, Jay." He didn't set the blond down. It was as if he couldn't. They whispered to each other. Brodie couldn't make out what was said. A tear slipped down the blond's beautiful face. Even though they looked nothing alike, except for their eyes, Brodie suspected this was the twin. He knew they had a bond. It had weighed on Cato being separated from the best half of himself. His words. Not Brodie's.

Finally, Cato set Callan on his feet. Callan swiped at his eyes while Cato and Jay hugged. Finally, Cato motioned Brodie's way. "This is Brodie. Brodie, my twin, Callan. I'm sure you know Jay, even if you haven't met."

Callan had a soft handshake. He blushed and backed into his husband's hold. "It's nice to meet you."

Jay reached around Callan and shook Brodie's hand. He was huge and over enthusiastic like a gigantic puppy. "You're Will West's son, right? The Chuckers' equipment manager?"

Brodie nodded. "That's me."

"Your dad was the absolute greatest."

Brodie smiled. "He still is."

Jay laughed. "That doesn't surprise me."

Cato checked his watch. "I don't want to rush anyone along, but the show is about to start." Brodie grabbed them each a Coke and moved to the living room. Several members of the team were scattered about, eating all Cato's snacks and putting their feet on the furniture. There were two seats left on the couch and a recliner. Jay dropped on the recliner before pulling Callan into his lap, leaving the couch to Cato and him. They sat side by side. Their thighs touched. Cato turned up the sound on the television as the show's intro started. He draped his arm across the back of the couch, over Brodie's shoulders, and leaned his way. Brodie swore he felt Callan's stare. Thankfully, the show started, engrossing everyone in the room.

Each time someone gasped or yelled, "Holy shit!" Cato and Brodie laughed. It had truly been a horrific experience, but also fun. Not to mention, that weekend had been the beginning of something amazing. When the hour ended, they got bombarded.

"I can't believe you two actually stayed three days." Brodie smiled at Gustav's words. He would've slept in a crypt for the nights he had with Cato that weekend.

Daire focused on Cato. "Do you believe in ghosts now?"

Cato snorted. "Fuck yeah. I thought I was going to die in that theater."

Everyone laughed. The crowd thinned as several players headed out to hit the bar. Soon, only Jay and Callan were left. Brodie set to work, cleaning up the team's mess. It was a habit. He carried an empty bowl to the sink. Cato's body molded against his back. His arms encircled Brodie's waist. He kissed the side of Brodie's neck.

"You're awful quiet tonight."

Brodie flashed a smile over his shoulder. "Nah. I'm just not as loud as everyone else."

A sexy chuckle rumbled against his ear. "Jay is always the loudest person in the room."

Damn. He wished they were alone. Unfortunately, he hadn't forgotten Cato's expression while he hugged his brother. "I'm about to head home and let you catch up with your brother."

"Are you sure?"

Brodie turned. Cato looked worried, as if he thought Brodie might be upset. He towed Cato down, luring him into a kiss. Their lips brushed. Brodie's heart filled with too much emotion to share. He breathed Cato's scent. "You haven't seen him in months. I'll still be here when he goes home."

Cato shuffled closer and stole a deeper kiss. When he pulled away, he openly struggled for air. "Damn. I miss you already."

A movement to their left startled them.

Cato turned his head but didn't jump away. Instead, he slowly released Brodie.

Callan blushed and looked everywhere but directly at them. "Sorry. I was just getting something to drink."

Another sexy chuckle rumbled from Cato. "It's fine."

Brodie stepped away. "It was really nice to finally meet you. I'm going to head home and let y'all visit."

Callan nodded, looking solemn. "It was really nice to meet you too. I can't tell you how happy I am someone cut out Cato's golfing habit."

Brodie looked Cato's way. His expression had closed. "You golf?"

"No."

Damn. He sounded pissed. Brodie was just confused. "Okay, well..."

Cato looked his way. His features softened. "I'll walk you out."

Brodie nodded. While he had no clue what secret message had just passed between the brothers, he would gladly take a few more minutes with Cato. He wanted all the kisses.

Cato took his time, saying his goodbyes. Inside, he fumed. Jay had sworn to him he would never tell Callan how he had faked golfing trips as an excuse to secretly sleep with men. He had promised to keep Cato's secrets. But Callan knew and there was only one way he could.

He waited until Brodie backed from the garage and the garage door closed behind him before heading back inside. Jay and Callan were cuddled on the couch, watching TV.

They looked up as Cato entered the living room. "He seems nice," Callan said, sounding sincere.

Jay joined in. "Will West's son? That's cool as hell. What's his dad like?"

Cato sat and stared at them, unsure of where to begin. His fury needed an outlet. His trust had been abused. He never lost his temper with Callan. Callan had suffered too much abuse in his life. Cato wouldn't add to it. He was his brother's protector.

Cato picked up a throw pillow and held it, trying to keep his anger inside. He cleared his throat. "How did you know about the golf?" His gaze stayed locked on Jay. He needed Jay to see the rage in his eyes.

Jay slightly shook his head, as if denying Cato's silent accusations without drawing attention to himself.

Callan laughed. "I'm not dumb, sweetie. You've never owned a set of golf clubs in your life." Cato's gaze shifted to Callan. Callan continued. "When you first started telling me that lie, I got worried you were up to something dangerous. I mean, you've never hidden anything from me. So I figured it had to be bad. I followed you one day."

Cato nodded. He didn't have to guess at what Callan had seen. "Why didn't you say anything?"

Callan held his stare, looking like the steady part of him he had always been. "It was yours. Your entire life, you've shared everything with me. This one time, it was yours."

Cato understood. Callan had said nothing because he was always amazing. He had chosen to let Cato have one thing he didn't have to share until he was ready to do so. Until he found the right person. His gaze moved Jay's way. He still thought Jay was funny and amazing, but he was amazing for Callan. Cato didn't love him. Likely, he never really had. Jay had just been safe. He had known Jay wouldn't love him back. Loving Jay let him stay hidden in his secrets. Seeing Jay again exposed every truth.

"Brodie is great, so is his family. I know you'll love him."

Callan smiled. "Yay. You two looked so in love when I walked in."

"That's because it's real." He hoped Jay understood. Cato had finally gotten things straight in his head. He didn't love Jay. Cato loved Brodie.

Sometimes, Brodie's house felt quiet and lonely. Because his dad was big on keeping Brodie safe, he had purchased Brodie a house down the street from him and in their gated community. The flip side of that was Brodie's house was huge. It was way too much for one person who would never have kids. Most of the rooms were empty. That made the house feel hollow sometimes. He liked Cato's house better. His house felt like a home. It was obvious he had taken care of someone else at some point and, being Callan's keeper, had taught him how to add something to his life Brodie hadn't captured. So Brodie paced.

The way Callan had blushed at catching them had so many questions running through his mind. Had even Cato's twin not known about his sexuality? Damn. He just felt so uneasy tonight. Brodie needed to schedule his next tattoo. He had been forced to cancel his appointment to get his second hand done. Since then, spending time with Cato had superseded everything. When Brodie felt twitchy, he always fell back on more ink. One of these days, he would run out of skin.

The doorbell rang, catching Brodie off guard. Not only was he not expecting anyone, but people also had to know the code to get past the gate. He headed for the door, expecting his dad. That was the only person who ever turned up unexpectedly. Brodie opened the door to find

Cato on the other side, holding a tiny teddy bear.

"Hey, gorgeous."

Brodie smiled so brightly his cheeks hurt. "Hey. I thought you were spending time with your brother."

Cato nodded. "I did. He went to bed, and I missed you."

How was he supposed to resist? Brodie took a step back, making room for Cato to pass. Once Brodie shut the door, Cato turned and handed him the bear. "For you."

Brodie stroked his tiny face. Even though he was a bear, he had raccoon features. "Where did you find this guy at this time of night?"

Cato looked guilty. "Actually, I already owned him. Callan and I sneaked out when we were sixteen. I stole my dad's car and took Callan to an arcade. Dad never let him do anything. I won that guy from a claw machine. The only time in my life I ever won at one of those things." Cato held his stare. "Just like you're the first time I've loved anyone."

Damn. Brodie thought he might actually cry. His throat swelled. He couldn't look away from Cato. Cato meant it. Brodie hugged the bear to his chest. "I love you too." The words fell so easily from his lips. Brodie couldn't deny the truth.

A sweet smile touched Cato's lips. "Can you please pack a bag and come home with me? I want you to know my family."

How was he supposed to resist?

CHAPTER NINE

IT FELT AMAZING HAVING Brodie tucked against his side on the couch first thing in the morning. They wore nothing but their pj pants. Callan and Jay were with them, doing the same. This was the life he had always wanted.

Callan looked Brodie's way. "I'm so glad you came back. I worried I wouldn't get a chance to know you."

Brodie made him proud. "Cato has told me so much about you. I couldn't miss my chance to hang out with the amazing twin he's always telling me about."

Cato watched the entire thing with love filling his chest. He had his favorite people all under one roof. Cato wished it could always be like this. He understood it couldn't.

"How long have you two been together?"

"Since June."

Callan looked surprised by Brodie's answer. "Wow. You must've met right after Cato moved."

Cato jumped in. "Brodie was damn near the first person I met here."

"Sounds like fate," Jay interjected.

It felt like fate. Cato hugged Brodie tighter and pressed his lips to Brodie's temple.

Brodie squeezed his thigh. Then he focused on Callan once more. "Cato tells me you're an amazing skater too. He says you could've been a figure skater if your family had invested even half of the effort they put into him into you."

Callan blushed and twisted his fingers. He didn't look at Brodie as he responded. "I don't know about that."

"As the team's equipment manager, I have access to the arena. Would you like to go skating?"

Callan's ears turned red. It was adorable when he turned this shy. "It's been a lot of years since I've been on the ice. I probably can't skate any longer."

Jay jumped in. "It's like riding a bike. Once you know, you never forget. I can hold you and keep you warm." The heat in Jay's voice couldn't be missed.

Cato couldn't look away from the way Jay watched Callan. There was so much love and lust in his eyes. Cato's throat swelled. Jay was exactly who Cato would have chosen for Callan. The way he spoke and treated Callan, that was all Cato had ever wanted for him. He hated himself for not being the brother Callan deserved since he married Jay. Cato needed to prove he could be better.

"We should go." At his comment, Callan looked his way and held his stare. Cato dug in. "I know you can do this. You're amazing at everything you do. If you're rusty, I know Jay will enjoy feeling you up as he keeps you upright. He would never let you fall."

Callan smiled. "Okay. I guess it would give Jay and you a chance to catch up too."

Cato nodded. "Exactly."

"I guess we should get ready," Callan said, coming to his feet.

Jay popped up behind him. He snatched Callan off his feet and tossed him over his shoulder. "We're going on a play date. We're going on a play date," he sang as he skipped down the hall, with Callan's peals of laughter following.

Brodie looked his way. "Don't even think about doing that to me."

Cato shook his head. "I have a different plan for you." He tackled Brodie, knocking him over so he could cover Brodie's body with his. Cato kissed Brodie like a starved man, because he was. He had waited twenty-three years for this amazing man. Now he couldn't get enough.

Brodie turned his head. "You're starting something you can't finish in a place where you definitely can't finish it."

Cato chuckled against Brodie's throat. "Nah. I'm just getting you warmed up for later."

"Cruel."

Cato licked Brodie's ear. "Maybe, but you love me anyway."

Brodie turned his head and met Cato's stare. His cheeks were flushed. He buried his fingers in Cato's hair. "You're damn right I do. With everything inside me."

Cato's eyes stung. He had never felt so cherished. "Same." And he wouldn't stop until his dying breath.

Each time Brodie thought Callan couldn't get cuter, he found a new level of adorableness. While dressed like he planned to play in the snow, Callan eased onto the ice. Brodie chuckled inside at the way Jay hovered. Cato was right. Jay would let nothing happen to his other half.

It didn't take long before Callan elegantly floated across the ice. He headed Brodie's way and snagged his arm. "Skate with me."

How could Brodie resist? He felt Cato's stare. Brodie looked his way. Cato looked intense. Brodie winked at him. A smile lit his face.

"You've changed him."

At Callan's comment, Brodie looked his way. "How so?"

He felt Callan shrug while holding his arm. "Cato has always been serious and brooding. With you, he smiles."

Brodie looked Cato's way again. Jay was hopping and skating around him, acting like a ballerina and being as dumb as possible. Cato only shook his head at the antics.

Brodie snorted. "Your husband is a mess."

"He's perfect."

Brodie's heart sighed at the love in Callan's voice. They were so pure and perfect for each other. Callan watched his husband with something beautiful in his eyes. It made Brodie wish they had more time together. Callan was obviously amazing.

Callan's gaze shifted his way, catching him staring. He blushed and looked away. "Cato and I had an ugly childhood. You can't know what it means for people like us to finally be shown real love. It's addictive and just everything."

Brodie hated to be nosey, but Callan had brought it up. "Cato told me your dad is in prison."

Callan nodded. "He hated me. Still does, I'm sure. He made my life a nightmare in every way. When Cato got picked up by the Ice Rockets, Dad worried it would ruin Cato's career when people learned he has a gay twin. So he shot me in the chest, just missing my heart. He honestly believed a tragic story about a dead twin would be beneficial to Cato's career. At his trial, he actually said if I had been a good brother, I would've died so Cato could thrive."

"Instead, Cato took you with him," Brodie surmised. "He loves you." Brodie couldn't focus on the ugliness of Callan's story. He couldn't imagine anyone being so cruel to Callan.

Callan smiled. "We were all we had. Until you and Jay came along. Cato and I hang on to the people who matter. He loves you. I can see it every time he looks at you." He squeezed Brodie's arm and nodded Jay and Cato's way. "He looks at you like Jay looks at me, and I can tell you, that's real love."

Brodie looked Cato's way. Callan was right. Jay and Cato wore matching expressions of complete adoration. Brodie's heart soared. He didn't doubt for a second Callan and he looked back at them, wearing the same expression. This was real.

Cato moved inside Brodie, thrusting and straining. They kissed while Cato made slow love to him. He wanted to keep Brodie in his bed forever. Sometimes he thought he might burst from his overwhelmed emotions. Brodie had been such a surprise to him. Just a wildly unexpected miracle in his darkest hour. Cato could never explain how cherished he was.

"Oh, God, Cato. Don't stop." Brodie strained against him, openly fighting his way toward orgasm. He bit Cato's shoulder, muffling his cry as his body tried stealing Cato's soul. Cum coated the space between them. Cato closed his eyes and focused on the building pressure. A gasp ripped from his throat as he finally blew. He didn't stop pumping inside Brodie until Brodie had drained every drop from him. Even then, he didn't pull out until his dick softened and slipped from Brodie's ass.

Brodie stroked Cato's chest and back. "Fuck. It's been the best day."

Cato nodded, brushing his nose against Brodie's with every dip of his chin. "I swear being with you gets better every damn day."

Brodie smiled even as he stole kisses.

Cato finally rolled away and tossed his condom in the bedside trash can. He snagged Brodie's waist and hauled him into his arms. Cato would worry about the mess later. Right now, he just wanted snuggles.

The air chilled their sweat-covered skin while Cato traced the back of Brodie's arm with his fingertips. He had no idea how much time passed before Brodie finally broke the silence.

"Callan told me what your father did. I know you told me your father tried to kill him, but damn."

"Honestly, that surprises me a little. He never talks about those days."

Brodie kissed his chest. "I think he just wanted to stress how amazing you are, which I already knew."

Cato smiled into the dark. "Or maybe he wanted to show you he likes and trusts you."

"I like him too."

Cato was beyond happy to hear it, since he didn't plan on letting Brodie go.

"I have a surprise for you."

That caught Cato's attention. Brodie had barely been out of his sight to plan any surprises. Still, an immediate burst of excited happiness rushed through him. No one ever did anything for him. "What?"

Brodie slipped from the bed. "Callan told me, when you two were kids, you had a secret place in the woods where you would sneak away to at night."

Cato laughed. He had honestly forgotten that. "Yeah. It was basically just a tarp thrown over some rope, looking like a half-assed tent."

Brodie dragged his overnight bag closer and threw it on the bed. "He also said you used to squirrel away money, lying to your parents about fake league fees, so you could buy snacks to eat around the campfire."

Cato had done that.

Brodie set his bag on the bed. "When I went home to get more clothes, I stopped by the store to grab some of the snacks he mentioned."

Cato rolled into a sitting position and eyed the bag as Brodie unzipped it. He couldn't stop smiling. "Really?"

Brodie nodded and started pulling snacks from his bag. He had stuff to make s'mores and Callan's favorite soda. "I thought, for his last night here tomorrow, we could light up the fire pit and have an impromptu camp out."

Pressure grew in Cato's chest. Each time he thought there were no more pieces of his heart left to steal, Brodie found more.

"You're wonderful."

Brodie shrugged. "Not really. I just love you and you love your twin. It's important he loves me too, because I never want to lose you."

Cato could barely swallow past the swelling in his throat. Brodie didn't have a thing to worry about. He didn't know Cato had never acted with anyone the way he had with Brodie. Cato had put everything out there and on the line. That's how much he believed in them. Brodie had nothing to fear. He was the one for Cato. Cato couldn't imagine ever loving anyone else.

CHAPTER TEN

CALLAN: *OMG! I LOVE Brodie so much. He's so perfect for you and I can't tell you how happy it made me to see you smiling. I can't wait until Christmas. It's been hard not having you around.*

Cato: *Brodie loves you too. He hasn't stopped raving about you. Brodie said you two exchanged numbers so you could plan Christmas together. You know whatever you decide, I'll be there.*

Callan: *Love you. Miss you already.*

Cato*: Same. Please text me when you land, so I know you made it.*

Callan: *I will.*

It was Cato's first tattoo. He had never been a fan before meeting Brodie. Seeing Brodie's tattoo-covered torso was the highlight of his day. He hadn't told Brodie. Brodie thought he needed to spend the day running errands. Cato wanted it to be a surprise. It was a small teddy bear with a raccoon face and the word "firsts" underneath. Brodie would know what it meant.

After this, he needed to go shopping for Brodie's Christmas present. He knew exactly what he wanted to get. It was something that had been nagging at the back of his mind.

"What are you doing after this?"

Cato looked Tommy's way at the question. The guy had been mostly quiet, hiding behind his hair. "Christmas shopping. This is probably my last chance. We have back-to-back games coming up and then I'm traveling to California for the holiday."

Tommy's gorgeous light green eyes met his stare for half a second. "Is that where your family lives?"

Cato forgot not everyone knew everything about him. That sounded vain in his head, but he rarely spent time in places where no one knew him. Honestly, it was kind of nice. "Yeah. My twin. I haven't seen him since Halloween. Brodie and I are heading out the twenty-third."

Tommy nodded. "Brodie has an appointment with me later too."

Cato nodded. "That's why I parked out back. I don't want him to see this until I'm ready. It's a surprise for him."

A slight smile touched Tommy's lips. "Don't worry. I won't tell him you were here."

"Thanks for that."

Tommy wiped his chest.

Cato eyed the final piece. "It looks great. Exactly like I pictured." His phone rang. Cato checked the face. It was Kieran. "Sorry, I have to take this."

"No problem. I'll give you care instructions when you're done."

With a nod, Cato popped from the chair and grabbed his shirt. He headed out back to take his call. Kieran only called about business. Sometimes that meant legal shit other people couldn't overhear.

"Hello?"

"You're invited to Christmas dinner after the game on the twenty-first."

A smile snapped to Cato's lips. It was just like Kieran not to say hi and to make immediate demands.

"Luckily for you, I don't have plans."

"There's never any luck involved with the things I do."

Cato chuckled at Kieran's curt tone. "Do I need to bring anything?"

"Just yourself. Henley and I have little family beyond my younger brother and his husband. We enjoy having friends around."

Cato touched his chest. He couldn't help it. For all Kieran's cold mannerisms, he was actually a great guy. Regardless of Kieran's claims about luck, Cato had gotten damn lucky to have him as an agent. "I'll bring wine."

Kieran blew out a sigh. "If you insist."

"And a gift for Henley."

"Whatever you need to do."

Cato's smile brightened. He knew he was getting under Kieran's skin. "And a gift for you."

"For fuck's sake."

Cato leaned against the back door, getting into the conversation. "What do I buy the man who has everything?"

Kieran scoffed.

Cato laughed. He didn't plan to end this call until Kieran hung up on him or said what he wanted.

Even though Brodie had an appointment to finally get his right hand tattooed, it felt strange not being with Cato. They were always together. He had a closet at Cato's house. A toothbrush. A life. He rarely went home any longer except to grab the mail. He wondered if it was unhealthy the way he missed Cato after only a few short hours apart. Brodie kept expecting these feelings to fade or at least weaken. It didn't happen.

First, Brodie shopped for Cato's Christmas present. He had the perfect gift in mind. Brodie had been musing over it for a while. Christmas had to be perfect. Then he headed for the mall to find something for Callan and Jay. He thought Callan would be the tough one to buy for, but it turned out to be Jay he couldn't think of a single thing to buy. The guy seemed like a giant child. That didn't mean he was into things like video games or whatever. He had no clue what to get. Finally, he gave up. He would text Callan later to get suggestions. Brodie had an appointment.

He headed to Masked Image with thoughts of Cato still racing through his mind. They felt so real. He hoped he wasn't setting himself up for heartache. It sounded strange, but he felt like they were too good to be true. He was so used to fighting and struggling in relationships; he didn't always know how to handle this calm love.

Brodie pulled into the parking lot. He took a minute, hiding Cato's gift. The last thing he wanted was for someone to smash in his window if they spotted the bag. With that out of the way, he stepped from his Jeep. He made it five steps be-fore Daire appeared at his side, startling the shit out of him.

"Hey, sexy."

Brodie jumped and grabbed his chest. "What the fuck, dude? Where did you even come from?"

Laughter swam in Daire's eyes. "I pulled in right behind you. Do you have an appointment today?"

Brodie nodded. "Things keep coming up, so I haven't had time to finish my right hand." He showed his hands and the way they didn't match.

"Cool. I have to put a deposit down on a new piece. That's why I'm here," Daire added, as if Brodie had accused him of something. Then Daire kept going, making it worse. "I'm not stalking you. Even though I would, if I thought it would make a difference."

Brodie rolled his eyes and picked up the pace. They had been on seemingly good terms for a while now. He didn't want that to change. Daire was one wrong word away from feeling Brodie's wrath. He opened the door. Daire was right on his heels.

Tommy opened his mouth, as if to greet him.

Daire refused to have any attention turned from him. "Just answer me one question. Why are you cool with staying a secret for Cato when you wouldn't do it for me?"

Uncomfortable, Brodie cast a glance at Tommy. Tommy kept his head down, doing his best to ignore them. Brodie decided there was no time like the present to put this to bed. "Because I'm not a secret with Cato. You know we're together. Everyone on the team knows we're together. Hell, even Tommy knows we're together."

To his surprise, Daire didn't chastise him for getting loud and dragging Tommy into things. Daire hated a scene. But as far as Brodie was concerned, Daire had started it.

Daire didn't back down or even look Tommy's way. "Yeah, the team knows, but the team loves you. You know that. That's not the same as the fans knowing, or him telling the world in an interview. You're still the secret. So tell me why that's suddenly okay with you now."

Brodie growled. "I don't need him to reveal my name in an interview or go on live TV and tell the world he's gay. Why would I give a fuck about strangers? He doesn't hide me in real life. The people who matter know I'm his. That's more than I can say about anyone else. It's definitely more than I ever got from you."

Daire took a step closer, getting visibly angry and obviously uncaring they had an audience. "And like I said, just because your friends know doesn't mean you're not still the secret. Yet I got dumped for this. So tell me why. I was damn good to you."

"Um, guys."

Brodie ignored Tommy. He was too angry to stop. "No. You absolutely weren't, and that's not what happened. I said I love you and you said, 'if you love me then you should be fine with being a secret.' I'm not. Did I hope you'd be jealous in the beginning with Cato? Yes, but—"

"Guys!"

At Tommy's shout, Brodie turned, ready to blast him too. Cato stood at his back. There was no way he had been standing there long. Still, he had obviously caught the worst of it. "Cato. I didn't know you were here. Your Hummer wasn't out front."

Cato's expression stayed completely blank, except for his eyes. His eyes looked dead. "That's because it's out back."

"It's not what you think," Daire said, making everything worse as far as Brodie was concerned.

"What do I think?"

No one answered. Brodie didn't know what Cato thought. It was bad, though.

Cato shifted from foot to foot. A muscle ticked in his jaw. Brodie couldn't decide if he planned to yell or fight. Instead, he chose something much worse. His voice came out calm. "I risked everything for you, and I didn't even hesitate the way I always believed I would. I hope Daire is worth losing us." He headed for the back door.

Brodie followed. "Hold up, Cato. I don't know what you heard, but let me explain."

Cato didn't stop. He climbed into his Hummer and slammed the door. Brodie tried opening it again, but it was locked. He had to jump back to keep his feet from getting run over as Cato immediately backed from his parking spot. Cato was gone before Brodie could blink.

Brodie stormed back inside. Fury burned in his soul. He swore his broken heart rattled with every step. "Did you get what you wanted?"

Daire looked oddly upset. He opened his mouth.

Brodie sliced his hand through the air. He didn't want to hear anything Daire had to say. "Don't fucking talk to me. Don't ever talk to me again. Everyone thinks you're this perfect guy who can do no wrong, but I know the real you. You're a fucking monster." Brodie stormed out, uncaring if he ever got his tattoo finished. Right now, he felt done with everything.

Daire stood in the middle of Masked Image with his heart in his throat. He hadn't meant for any of that to happen. Part of him felt like he should go after Brodie, but he recognized that would only make things worse. He hadn't meant to lose his temper. It was just that questions had been eating at his mind since Brodie started dating Cato. He couldn't see that Cato did anything different than he had. Well, for the most part. He hadn't stayed faithful. But Daire hadn't thought Brodie expected it until he caught Daire with Gustav. He hadn't held Brodie's hand around the team or shown him any preferential treatment. But Daire had gone to restaurants and whatnot with Brodie.

He imagined those outings looked like two friends out to dinner. Still, that was exactly how Cato and Brodie looked to the public. Why was is it different?

"It looks like I have an open appointment."

Without a word, Daire peeled off his shirt and sat. They had already discussed what he wanted. Daire paid him and sat back, hoping for the pain. It was what he deserved. Brodie wasn't wrong about everything. Daire should have reacted differently when Brodie had admitted to loving him. He had panicked. Daire wasn't ready to settle down. Hell, sometimes he didn't know what the fuck he wanted. But damn, Daire had loved Brodie in his own way, as much as he could love anyone. Each time they saw each other—since the day Brodie said he was done—Brodie had turned cold. He showed no emotion to Daire. Brodie acted like they were mere acquaintances. Every time, the knife dug deeper into his heart. He recognized he had discovered his conscience too late, but damn. He honestly did have one. Brodie should have given him a chance to prove it. He should have at least let him explain.

"Cato just got a tattoo as a surprise for Brodie."

Daire turned his head at Tommy's soft-spoken words.

Tommy's gorgeous light green eyes focused on him, holding Daire captive. "He told me the story behind it. It was adorable. You just fucked up something special."

Daire looked away. "I know. That's what I do."

Tommy would know. He was also on the long list of people Daire had fucked over with his bullshit. Daire didn't know why he couldn't stop. Maybe he was just a bad person.

CHAPTER ELEVEN

NOTHING FELT RIGHT ANY longer. Cato played. He did all the things he had been hired to do. That was it. He no longer stayed after each game until Brodie finished working. In fact, he got out of there as quickly as possible. That was doubly true tonight. He had to be at Kieran's place in an hour. Cato couldn't dawdle.

"Can I walk out with you so we can talk?"

Cato glanced Daire's way at the quietly spoken question. Rage poured through him. "You've got nothing to say to me." Cato walked away before he acted on the rage that lived in his heart. No one understood. When he had moved to New Orleans, he had just let hiding his sexuality break his heart. He had been dead set no one would ever know about him. Not that he was ashamed. Cato's twin had almost died because of this career. That was how much his brother had sacrificed so Cato could get to the top. He had always believed he couldn't let his career be defined by his sexuality. Not to mention he had seen the way Callan had been treated.

Then Cato had met Brodie. There had never been a decision to make. He cared more about Brodie than anything else.

For once, he had found something bigger than his fears. He never would have hidden Brodie. But he guessed he was just a cover or a substitute for the man Brodie really loved. The man who was ashamed to love him. Sometimes nobody won. More times than not, it was Cato.

He drove to Kieran's on autopilot. Cato couldn't think of anything he wanted to do less than to fake smile and make nice. He wanted to go home and wallow, the way he had done every night since losing Brodie. Each time he closed his eyes, he heard Brodie admitting to loving Daire and hoping their relationship made Daire jealous. That was all he had meant. Cato was the biggest of fools.

As he arrived at Kieran's, Cato grabbed the bottle of wine he had bought for the occasion and the sparkling apple cider

Kieran suggested for Henley. It turned out Henley was a recovering addict. Cato felt like he should have known that or had heard that somewhere. He had forgotten since Henley seemed so healthy now. Cato headed for the door with his heart in his throat. He didn't want to watch them loving each other while he had nothing. Cato was still raw.

A man Cato had never seen answered the door. He smiled like the sweetest of angels. "Hi. You must be Cato."

Despite himself, Cato smiled. The man's voice was soft. He brought out something protective in Cato. "I am."

The man waved him inside. "I'm Gannon. Kieran's brother."

Cato nodded. "It's nice to meet you." He held out the bottles he had brought. "Wine and sparkling cider, as promised."

A hulking blond who looked somewhat familiar appeared from nowhere. "I'll take those."

Gannon flashed the man a loving but exasperated-looking smile. "Rude." His laughing gaze returned to Cato. "That's my husband, Alex."

With a first name and face, it hit Cato. Alex Cormier played minor league. He was known for his ruthlessness on the ice. It seemed odd to realize he had such a seemingly sweet husband.

Gannon motioned for Cato to follow. "Everyone is in the family room. I think we're waiting for one more guest before we eat. Would you like a drink?"

Cato tried like hell to keep up a brave face. "Sure. What are my options?"

Rather than name everything, Gannon led Cato to a table laden with various drinks. Cato picked a nonalcoholic beverage and made his way to Kieran to say hello. To Cato's surprise, Kieran was deep in conversation with Gustav. The sexy Swede, who had fan fiction dedicated to him, smiled as he spotted Cato.

"You move slow tonight."

"Or you drive too fast," Cato said, accepting the man's handshake like they hadn't just come from the same place.

Kieran eyed him. "How are you?"

His kindness blindsided Cato. For a moment, he couldn't breathe. He couldn't handle anyone seeing him too clearly right now. "I'm fine." It was a complete lie, but what else was he supposed to say?

Kieran squeezed his shoulder. His gaze moved past Cato. "Excuse me. My husband needs me."

Left alone, Gustav's demeanor changed from congenial to concerned. "How are you really? Daire told me what happened."

Cato wanted to throw punches at only the sound of Daire's name. The rage was twice as thick, knowing Daire was out there spreading the gossip. "I can't imagine what he had to say."

Gustav shrugged. "He said he confronted Brodie out of stupid jealousy. You heard only part of the conversation, and not the part where Brodie ripped him a new one. He guessed you hadn't known about their past and was more than a little angry to learn the way you did. I admit I don't understand why this led to your breakup. It's been almost two years since they were together. They've found a way to be civil, but Daire is the only one who isn't over it. When Brodie was done, he was done. That's just who he is."

Cato didn't know how to feel. He had heard what he had heard. Brodie had said he loved Daire and wanted to make him jealous. Right?

"Now that everyone's here, we can move to the dining room."

At Kieran's words, Cato turned. There he was, hovering in the doorway, looking unsure of his welcome. There were dark circles under his eyes. Cato's heart squeezed.

"I know you aren't children, but you have assigned seats. Please look for your name. At least two people have allergies. We don't want to have to break out the epi-pens tonight."

Before Cato made it to the dining room, he already knew. They were seated next to each other. Just like Kieran's dirty trick with the one room with one bed situation, Kieran could not stop meddling.

Cato didn't argue. He sat. They were adults. It was just one dinner. No matter what, they would have to see each other. That was the bed they had made by mixing business with pleasure. They reached for the same folded cloth napkin. Their hands brushed.

"Sorry," Brodie muttered, pulling his hand away.

Cato could barely breathe. He looked Brodie's way. For a moment, their gazes met. Brodie looked as broken as Cato felt. Cato turned away. Confusion ate him alive.

Kieran gave a speech about found family and how important it was to share these moments. Cato didn't hear half of it. Food appeared in front of him. He picked at it. People spoke all around them. Neither Brodie nor Cato said a word. Then something odd happened. Their knuckles brushed beneath the table. Then their fingers linked. It was almost mutual—like Cato had no clue who initiated the move. It was as if they decided together to move past their first big issue. He recognized he maybe should have let Brodie explain. Cato wasn't over it, but he loved Brodie. He needed to give him a chance.

Brodie's soul cried the moment their fingers had linked. He fought back tears. No matter how he turned things in his head, he didn't know what words to use to fix them. But Cato met him halfway and Brodie's heart needed this settled. The moment they could slip away unnoticed, Brodie focused on Cato.

"Can we talk?"

Cato nodded.

Together, they stood and headed for the door. When the cool night air washed over him, Brodie shivered. Cato removed his dinner jacket and draped it over

Brodie. The material swallowed him. It was warm and smelled like Cato. A tear fell without his permission. He wiped it away on the sly. Brodie had always considered himself a strong person. Losing Cato had tested that belief.

Brodie didn't know where to start, so he kept moving until he reached his Jeep. He unlocked the door and dug through the console until he found what he needed. Brodie turned and handed Cato a small plastic bag.

"I bought this for you for Christmas. You can check the date and time on the receipt. I bought it before... everything."

Cato opened the bag and checked the receipt before flipping open the velvet box.

He blinked at the contents. "What's this?" Cato didn't lift his head. It was as if he couldn't look away from the circle of platinum and diamonds inside.

"It's an engagement ring. I'd planned to ask you to marry me on Christmas Eve. Your brother was helping me plan the perfect surprise proposal for you." Brodie took an unsteady breath and pushed on. "I needed you to see this ring, so maybe I can make you understand you're the man I want. You're the only man I love." He made a helpless gesture. Brodie didn't know what words to say. "I was so fucking mad at Daire that day. He confronted me, wanting to know why I would stay with you while you kept me a secret, while I hadn't been willing to do the same for him."

"I never kept you a secret."

The same outrage filled Brodie as it had that day. "Exactly! That's what I said, but he kept insisting that just our friends knowing wasn't the same as publicly claiming me. That you were no better than he had been. I was so goddamn mad because you are everything he's not. His sheer nerve to compare you two when I love you so goddamn much." Tears fell and Brodie couldn't stop them. He tried swiping at his face. "I don't know when you walked in or what you heard, but I would never, ever choose anyone over you. You're the one for me. I wanted so fucking badly to marry you. How can you just..." Brodie's hands rose and fell. He didn't understand how Cato could walk away from them. They had been so beautiful.

"Wanted?"

Confusion had Brodie's brow furrowing. "What?"

"You said you wanted to marry me. Do you not want to marry me anymore?"

Brodie stopped breathing.

Cato didn't stop there. "Because I still want to marry you. I sent Callan the money to buy you the perfect ring, since he has better taste than me. He was also helping me come up with ideas for the perfect surprise proposal for Christmas. I guess the surprise Callan had planned was we both planned to propose."

"You still want to marry me?" Brodie swore he heard every word Cato said, but those were the ones he couldn't get past.

"Of course. I love you. If we can't get past this misunderstanding, then I guess we have no business getting married. But I believe in us, and I love you too much to let you go."

For a moment, all Brodie could do was stare at Cato. Then his feet moved. Cato's arms wrapped around him. Their lips met. Brodie couldn't stop crying. It was so ridiculous. He wasn't a crier, but losing Cato had broken him like nothing ever had before.

Cato wiped away his tears. "Please don't cry, baby. I should've given you a chance to explain. You deserved that. I was just so caught off guard. All I heard was you saying you loved him and you wanted him to be jealous. It was like getting punched in the chest. Since we met, you've been my every thought. I didn't know I could love someone so deep. But maybe I expected it was too good to be true, and it was almost like a self-fulfilling prophecy or some shit. I can't lose you."

Brodie took the box from Cato. He dropped to one knee. "This isn't the romantic proposal I had planned, but this is a sincere one. Please marry me. I can't go through another week like this last one. It's unnatural for us to be apart."

Cato pulled him to his feet. "I think I already said yes, but yes." He held Brodie so tightly, he couldn't breathe. Brodie didn't care. He didn't need oxygen. "Come home with me. Follow me there and let me make up for everything."

Brodie swiped at his cheeks. "Okay. First, put the ring on." He had to see his ring on Cato's finger. Brodie wouldn't be sure they were okay until he did.

With a nod, Cato let Brodie slip the ring on his hand. He took an unsteady breath. The ring looked perfect. It looked like Cato would soon be his.

CHAPTER TWELVE

HE DROVE HOME WITH his stomach shaking. So much had happened between Brodie and him. He didn't want to think. All Cato had done was think for the past week. He hadn't slept and barely eaten. His mind had been a twenty-four-hour-a-day spiral. There were still tiny things he wasn't fully over. It still bothered him Brodie had wanted Daire to be jealous. But, at the end of the day, they had just gotten together back then, and their feelings hadn't been what they were now. It was a tough pill to swallow, but it was also reality. Brodie loved him and only him now. That was all that mattered.

When they pulled into his garage, parking side by side, some of the shaking subsided. It felt right for Brodie to be parked next to him—like this was their home. Realistically, he knew Brodie owned a much nicer house and would likely want to live there. Tonight, this house was theirs in his heart.

As they each stepped from their vehicles, their gazes met. Brodie headed straight for him. Without a word, they linked fingers and headed inside the house. Cato didn't stop moving until they were inside his bathroom. The chill inside him needed warmth. He had a feeling Brodie felt the same. They didn't speak. Cato started them a bath and added bubbles. They undressed as if it was their nightly routine. Cato's spine didn't relax until Brodie sat between his legs and leaned against his chest, soaked in hot water.

With his arms wrapped around Brodie, Cato kissed his neck. "I had a thought as we pulled into the garage. It seemed so natural to see your vehicle parked next to mine—like we were coming home. It made me realize you'd probably prefer if we moved to your place since it's bigger."

"Actually, no," Brodie said, surprising him. Their fingers linked. Cato watched bubbles run down Brodie's arm. Brodie spoke, breaking the spell. "I remember when I went home Halloween night so you could spend time with Callan. As I came through the door, it felt like I was at a stranger's house. Maybe it's because you're here. I don't know, but this place feels like home. If you'd rather live in my house, that's cool too. My home is wherever you are. This place is just where I fell in love with you, I guess."

Cato understood. This was where most of their memories had been made.

"How will your dad feel about you giving up the house he bought for you?"

He felt Brodie shrug. "Honestly, he'll probably be thrilled because I'm doing it for you. He never stops raving about how impressed he is with your bravery. How anyone strong enough to not be ashamed in your profession was strong enough to take care of his boy. He likes you."

Cato smiled against Brodie's shoulder. "The feeling is mutual."

He had gone into meeting Brodie's parents with a bit of awe. It turned out Brodie's dad was more than the legend everyone knew him to be. He was a dad. The man was definitely the dad Cato had never had. He was slightly jealous of the childhood Brodie must've had.

He turned their joined hands so he could look at the ring on his finger. Cato wasn't surprised it fit perfectly. It was Brodie's job to pay attention to the details, and he was very good at his job.

"I can't wait until we get to California so you can have your ring."

"A part of me really resents that our plans were ruined. I can't imagine how excited Callan must've been, knowing we both planned to propose. That strikes me as the kind of thing that would tickle him to death."

Cato couldn't stop brushing his lips across Brodie's shoulder. His love needed an outlet. "Maybe we can still salvage things."

"I'm listening."

Cato smiled at the open curiosity in Brodie's voice. "Instead of an engagement party, let's get married. I know your parents were disappointed we wouldn't be with them for Christmas. Ask if they're willing to come to California with us." The more he spoke, the more the idea grew on Cato. "Callan would gladly add them to our Christmas celebration. While we have everyone in place, we could have a gorgeous Christmas-themed wedding."

Brodie didn't speak.

Cato fought the urge to laugh nervously and tell him never mind. Instead, he squeezed Brodie. "Why are you so quiet? You can tell me no."

Brodie sniffed and Cato realized he was silently crying again.

Cato held him tighter. "What's wrong, baby? Talk to me."

"Once you marry me, the entire world will know. I didn't really think about it when I planned my proposal, but now it feels real. People will call you names and everyone will talk about your performance on the ice, using a scale of how gay you are. That'll be my fault."

"I don't give a fuck about any of that." As the words burst from him, Cato recognized how true they were. More than that, he realized he didn't care at all about his career when comparing it to being with Brodie. "I would rather retire tomorrow than not be married to you. My whole life, I've worried about everything you just listed. In fact, I've spent my entire life doing everything for everyone else's sake. Now that I have you, none of that shit factors at all. I'd rather have you. You're the one thing that's just for me."

Brodie turned and straddled Cato's lap. His nose and eyes were red. He was beautiful. "I love you. If you're serious, then I'd love a beautiful—and very small—Christmas wedding." Something flickered across his features, as if a thought hit.

Cato squeezed his ass. "What? What was that look?"

"The team. They'll be upset they weren't invited."

Cato shrugged. "So invite them. If they can make it out to California, great. If not, we tried. But this is supposed to be about us, so don't start stressing about everyone else. I want to marry you, but it'll have to be what we can throw together in a few days. We can't worry about anyone else."

Brodie smiled. "That's true."

His gaze dropped, obviously taking in Cato's new tattoo for the first time. Brodie's finger hovered over it, as if he wanted to trace it, but he recognized it was still healing. His gaze lifted. He looked how Cato felt—like he was constantly wowed by finding his other half. "I love you."

The way the words came out in a whisper somehow felt more powerful than if he had yelled. Cato's throat swelled. "I love you too."

Brodie shook his head. His eyes looked devastated. "I can't imagine how I made you feel right on the heels of doing this." He sounded wrecked. "I never meant to fail you."

Cato couldn't have that. He stood, bringing Brodie with him. Soaked and with bubbles streaming down their bodies, he carried Brodie to bed. Cato covered Brodie's body with his as he took him down on the mattress.

"Never say that to me again. You didn't fail at shit. It was just a dumb miscommunication. No one is more loved than you. I will always find my way back to you."

With that vow still hovering on his lips, he claimed Brodie's mouth. If Brodie didn't understand yet how far Cato would go to hang on to them, he would have to show him.

Cato was so big. He was everywhere. Going from the hot bath to a cool room might have had him freezing, except there was no way with Cato kissing him. His body was on fire. So much love filled his heart, Brodie thought he might explode. He had been so fucking terrified he would never get to hold Cato again. Brodie had watched him on the ice the past two games. Cato's features had matched the frozen liquid beneath his skates. Brodie felt his hatred. It was so much worse than anything Brodie had ever experienced. Until he lost Cato, Brodie hadn't realized he had never truly loved before Cato. What they had was powerful. Brodie would do anything to keep it.

"I need to get inside you. My heart needs it."

Brodie understood. He didn't give a fuck about foreplay. His heart needed the connection too. "Hurry."

Cato snagged the lube from where he kept it stashed. With the bare minimum of prep, Cato pushed his way inside. Brodie's breath stuttered.

Cato went still.

They held each other's stare. Then Cato rocked against him. Brodie thought he might cry again. Fuck. He had no idea what was wrong with him. Brodie had never been this emotional. Almost losing Cato for good had broken something inside him. He couldn't stop shaking inside.

"I can't wait to be your husband."

The words had tears slipping back into Brodie's hair. Cato was everything he ever wanted. That fucking tattoo. God. He was wrecked.

"Same." Brodie pulled him down for a kiss. He just needed. That was it. He was a ball of pure need.

Their tongues fought. Cato drove his lust higher by the second. Brodie didn't want to come. He wanted Cato to stay inside him forever. If they were connected for eternity, then he could never lose him again. Cato didn't give him that choice. He played Brodie's body like a master. Cato knew him. He knew how to drive him insane.

The pressure built. Their kiss turned wild. Brodie's short fingernails tore at Cato's skin, trying desperately to get closer. Sounds came from the back of his throat he couldn't control. The tension became too much. Like a spring, he snapped. His body shook. He cried out against Cato's mouth as jets of cum coated his stomach. Cato didn't stop pounding, forcing every wave of pleasure from him. When Cato blew, he stared at Brodie, never breaking eye contact. For a moment, Brodie felt like the world disappeared. It was only them. Sometimes, that was exactly what he wanted.

Too soon, Cato cleaned their skin. Brodie felt lost until Cato dragged him into his arms and cuddled him hard. Brodie couldn't stop kissing any skin he could reach. Cato's fingertips trailed up and down his skin. They felt perfect.

"How does Gustav know about Daire and you?"

Brodie's gaze shot to Cato's face. He definitely didn't want to talk about Daire, but he equally needed to know where the question came from. "Why?"

He felt Cato shrug. "At dinner tonight, Gustav said he didn't understand why I had walked away from you over Daire when you two were over two years ago. I've just been wondering how he knows any of that."

Brodie stacked his hands on Cato's chest and held his stare. "Gustav knows about Daire because I walked in on them fucking when Daire was supposed to be with me. I never blamed Gustav. That's the thing with Daire. He's not scared of anyone knowing he's gay. Not really. It's just a game. He makes people believe that so he can fuck as many people as he wants while none of them know about each other. Gustav knows what happened between you and me because he found me crying after the game before last. He wouldn't leave until I told him everything."

"It's strange," Cato said, sounding sad. That had Brodie's attention. "Daire seems so nice—like everyone loves him. I really liked him. Hell, Gustav and him are always together. I would've never guessed he had hurt him too. But when I look back on things, there were a few times I thought Daire might be flirting with me, but I blew it off as being impossible. Since everything happened, it's made me wonder if he hoped to drive a wedge between us."

Brodie snorted. "More likely than not, he was just hoping to fuck you too. As for Gustav, Daire can't hurt him. He's in love with someone else."

"It's not you, is it?"

Brodie snorted. "No."

Cato squeezed his ass. "Good. I don't want to fight everyone. I mean, I will, but I'd rather not."

Brodie kissed his chest. "Don't worry. No one can compete. What does my ring look like?"

Cato laughed. He rolled, pinning Brodie beneath him. "Nice subject change and good try, but you have to wait."

Brodie stuck out his bottom lip, pouting. Cato nibbled it.

"Nu-uh. None of that. I can keep you distracted, but you have to wait."

"You don't know what it looks like either, do you?"

Cato goosed his side. "Of course, I know. Quit trying to goad me into telling you."

Brodie wrapped his arms around Cato's neck and drew him closer. "Maybe I just wanted you to get annoyed enough to end up right where you are." He lifted his head and bit Cato's bottom lip.

Cato groaned. "Damn. You plan to be the death of me, don't you?"

In a way, that was exactly what Brodie planned. He would be at Cato's side until death parted them. It looked like the brightest of futures.

Chapter Thirteen

Brodie couldn't stop staring at the rings on his finger. They were perfect and God only knew how much Cato had dropped on them. His face hurt from smiling. Most of the team had made it to the wedding despite it being a holiday. It helped they played in San Diego the day after Christmas. Brodie purposely tried not to see Daire, who had also come. They couldn't invite the entire team without inviting Daire. It would have made people talk.

They didn't want that. It was their special day.

Thankfully, something they hadn't considered until Kieran dove into their contracts, there had been nothing contractually stopping them from getting married. Brodie would have quit if there had been. That was how dedicated he was to Cato. But it hadn't been an issue.

Cato. Brodie's heart sighed. He looked gorgeous, decked out in a tux while chatting with Brodie's dad. They both smiled, as if enjoying each other's company. Brodie was so fucking in love. It had been such a beautiful Christmas wedding. He felt like he lived in a dream. Callan had thrown together a gorgeous wedding with little to no time to get it done.

Daire appeared from nowhere. "Can we talk?"

"No." Brodie wouldn't let his mood be ruined.

"I just need to apologize. It's important to me."

Before Brodie responded, Jay appeared. With his arm around Daire's shoulders, he flashed a feral smile as he steered Daire away. "Let's have a talk about boundaries."

Callan sidled up next to him and put his arm around Brodie's waist. Brodie draped his arm over Callan's shoulders. It felt good—like he had a brother.

"I'm so happy."

Brodie smiled at Callan's claim. He sounded happy. "Me too."

"I've never seen Cato smile this much. You worked a miracle on him. Before he moved, I'd gotten really worried about him. It was like he had fallen into a black hole and couldn't climb out. Then he met you and I think you saved him."

Brodie was more moved than he could express, but he also had a confession of his own. "He saved me too. I'd given up on anyone openly loving me." Brodie made a helpless gesture. "He shook me from my shell."

Callan nodded, looking solemn. "That's what it was like to meet Jay. He kind of barged in and refused to leave."

A bark of laughter burst from Brodie. He could see Jay doing that. Cato appeared with two glasses of champagne and a champagne glass filled with Coke.

Brodie laughed at the sight of it. Cato really knew him. He hated the taste of alcohol.

Cato handed Callan a glass of champagne and Brodie the Coke. "I can't tell you how happy it makes me to see the two greatest loves of my life together."

Callan beamed.

The way Callan always lit beneath his twin's attention warmed Brodie's heart. It couldn't have been more obvious, he thought Cato hung the moon. It also couldn't have been more obvious, the only reason Callan hadn't been completely starved of love his whole life was because Cato loved him more than an entire family could. That said everything about Cato, as far as Brodie was concerned. He was good all the way to his soul. Cato's gaze moved Brodie's way.

"Is it okay if I steal my husband? According to Brodie's mom, it's time for the first dance."

Callan straightened away. "Oh. I should go find Jay."

The first strum of music filled the air.

Jay appeared like a ninja. "I'm here. Don't dance with anyone else." He sounded out of breath—as if he really had pulled some sick moves to get to Callan before anyone else.

Callan laughed as Jay dragged him toward the ballroom. They had been lucky to snag a gorgeous wedding spot for the day. Brodie had a feeling his dad had greased some palms to convince the owners to work on the holiday.

Cato set their glasses aside and took Brodie's hand. He lifted it to his lips. His gaze screamed Cato would do naughty things to him later. Then, together, they headed inside the ballroom. No one could start dancing until they did. As Brodie stepped onto the dance floor, Cato swept him into his arms. Cato's sexy familiar scent washed over him. Brodie closed his eyes and lost himself in Cato's hold.

Tomorrow, Cato would play San Diego, and then they would start their honeymoon. They were going to another haunted hotel to investigate with the *Spectral* team. Brodie couldn't wait. Cato couldn't either. Nothing could have proven more he had found his person. Brodie would never let him go.

Keep an eye out for the next Thin Ice, *Pucking Screwed*.

Please consider leaving a review at the retailer where you purchased this book. Reviews really help with a book's visibility, which allows me to continue writing more stories. Thank you, Charity.

About the Author

CHARITY PARKERSON IS AN award-winning and multi-published author with several companies. Born with no filter from her brain to her mouth, she decided to take this odd quirk and insert it in her characters. One of her greatest loves is writing morally gray characters. You'll find them scattered throughout her hundreds of titles.

*Eight-time Readers' Favorite Award Winner

*2015 Passionate Plume Award Finalist

*2013 Reviewers' Choice Award Winner

*2012 ARRA Finalist for Favorite Paranormal Romance

*Five-time winner of The Mistress of the Darkpath

Connect with her online:

*Sign up for her newsletter: https://send fox.com/charityparkerson

*Join her readers' group on Facebook: http://bit.ly/CharitysTribe

*Website: https://www.charityparkerso n.com

*A list of her social media accounts and giveaways all in one place: http://hy.pag e/charityparkerson

www.ingramcontent.com/pod-product-compliance
Lightning Source LLC
Chambersburg PA
CBHW060436180626
46817CB00007B/2837